By Jack Gantos
Published by Farrar, Straus and Giroux

The Jack Henry Books

Heads or Tails: *Stories from the Sixth Grade*
Jack's New Power: *Stories from a Caribbean Year*
Jack's Black Book

For Young Adults

Desire Lines

Jack's Black Book

Wood shop is killing me. Today I was using the electric jigsaw so I could carve Beau-Beau's name out of an old pine board I found on the back of Dad's truck. Well I was nervous using it because I had never used one before and I was paying real close attention until Mr. Gilette snuck up on me from behind and yelled, "Henry, you nitwit!" I turned to look at him and the saw went out of control and did a little jig across my fingers. And it hurt like having my hand slammed in a car door and the blood spurted out all over my face and on Mr Gilette's hat

1 2 3 4 5
Q T
A D F

and he went nutty and started yelling
at me and I got nervous and grabbed
the dancing saw but it jerked away
from me and somehow it stayed on
and I kept trying to grab the
trigger but my hands were slippery
with blood and the only thing at
that moment I could think about
was murder. Like a murder mystery
novel where a real demented sicko
takes a saw and chops up his
victims. [illegible] fingers and
toes would be difficult but just
think how hard [illegible] be to
saw through a leg or a neck or
a belly. But if I was writing the book
my character would be tough and cool

JACK'S BLACK BOOK

Jack Gantos

Farrar, Straus and Giroux
New York

Distributed in Canada by Douglas & McIntyre Ltd.
Printed in the United States of America
Designed by Caitlin Martin
First edition, 1997

12 11 10 9 8 7 6 5

Library of Congress Cataloging-in-Publication Data
Gantos, Jack.
Jack's black book / Jack Gantos. — 1st ed.
p. cm.
Summary: Comic misadventures ensue when seventh-grader Jack tries to write the great American novel.
ISBN 0-374-33662-8
[1. Authorship—Fiction. 2. Humorous stories.] I. Title.
PZ7.G15334Jab 1997
[Fic]—dc21 96-53107

For Mabel Grace

Contents

was the last to know that these kind of Cocker Spaniel dogs had thier brains bred out of them a long time ago so they would be really stupid and just lay around the house all day but our Beau-Beau was like an experiment gone bad, as if Doctor Frankenstien had made him from a bunch of different dog pieces he found at a vet's office. He had the giant paws of a Great Dane and the brain of a Chichuahua. Once he was desperate to go outside and he went out the little cat rubber door and got stuck half way through. Unfortunately his back half was still inside the house so he pooped on

PART ONE

Go Dog Go, or How I Passed the Seventh Grade

the rug. When we found him we tried to pull him out b[illegible] wa[illegible] so dad had to get some grease he used to pack wheel bearings and we slathered it all over Beau-Beau's fur. We gave him a tug by his hind legs. He yelped really loud but he did make it through the opening. [illegible] had to give a [illegible] and that took forever because the grease was so hard to get out. ugh! [illegible] think what [illegible] remember most about Beau-Beau was the way he would eat any kind of bugs. Pete used to feed him any kind of big juicy Palmetto bug and he would snap it

Slim Jack
25¢
SPICY
SMOKED
SNACK
ingredients: [illegible]at, pig nose, pig butt, pig eyes, ears + toe
Jack
Slim

WE LOVE YOU

One

It was pitch-black in my room and as I wrote I tried to imagine the size of each letter so I could keep the words in line and read what I had written in the light of morning. But no matter how carefully I wrote I knew my words would be jumbled and piled up over each other like train cars that had jumped the tracks. It didn't matter if I could read the words or not. I knew what I was thinking when I wrote them. They were the same discouraging thoughts in the light of day or in the middle of the night. I had the words memorized from saying them to myself over and over again as I walked down the street, or opened a book, or tried to write. *Moron. Idiot. Stupid.* Two weeks earlier I had received my aptitude-test scores from school and since then I had been giving myself a hard time. Now I could feel myself reaching the end of my rope.

After another restless night I rolled out of bed and held

the curtain to one side. It was just purple enough over the Teeters' roof to know it was time to get ready for school. Pete was still asleep on his side of the room. I wanted to sneak over there and strangle him. The night before, he said it was a good thing I was brain dead because if I was ever in the army and captured, the enemy could torture me all they wanted and I'd still have nothing to confess.

I looked down at the floor. My personal diary was open to the page I had last written. It looked like the scratching of a madman just moments before he did something he could never take back. If I threw myself off the Intercoastal bridge and drowned, everyone would think they knew why once they read what I'd been writing. They'd say things like, "Poor kid had low self-esteem." Or, "He didn't get enough positive reinforcement." But they'd be missing the point. Calling myself an idiot wasn't about receiving enough gold stars or pats on the head. This was about scientific proof that I was dumb. Slow. Dim. Mentally challenged. A born, biological, stone-cold *loser.*

Right next to my personal diary was my new writer's journal. It was totally blank. Not a pencil scratch. Hardly a fingerprint. I bought the plain black book with unlined pages because I had decided to write a novel. I had made up my mind to become a writer, so I figured, why wait until I'm old? Write a novel now, make some money, and move from Fort Lauderdale to Paris or New York or Dublin, where all the famous writers live interesting lives. But I didn't know how to write a novel. I didn't know what my characters were like. I didn't know the setting. I didn't have a plot, or a theme, or even a beginning, middle, or end. I didn't have a clue—yet. I was still waiting for a good idea to strike me. I had read in an old writers' magazine that authors, when they were stuck, sometimes just needed to sit around in their bathrobes and stare dreamily up at the ceiling. Until, suddenly, an angel called a writer's "muse" would descend and whisper inspirational ideas into their ears. Then bingo, their pens begin to move across the pages like the pointer on a Ouija board. But the more I stared at the cracks in my ceiling while dressed in a terry-cloth bathrobe, sucking on my lead pencil point with my ears perked up like a Chihuahua's, the only ideas that rolled around my empty head were ugly. *Give up. Throw in the towel. You don't have what it takes to write a novel.* My stupidity was stalking me like some big dumb monster with a club. Every time I thought I was smart enough to write, WHAM, I'd get smacked across the side of the head. And the more I whaled on myself, the dumber I felt, and the more it paralyzed me. I hadn't written the first word, but I hadn't given up hope.

What encouraged me to stick with writing was this one weird thing: whenever I closed my eyes, the letters of the alphabet shifted around like Scrabble pieces and formed words. Those words lined up and soon I imagined entire pages of writing so clearly that I could actually read them, sentence after sentence, as if I were reading straight from a book. A book I had written, with my name on the cover and my stories inside. I could feel the weight of that book in my open hands and inhale the clean smell of ink and paper when I stuck my nose between the pages. I could imagine looking through a bookshop window and seeing a stack of my books on display. "Yes," I'd hiss. "The idiot did it! The moron has triumphed! Those are mine." And I'd be so dizzy with pride I'd stumble down the road as weak-kneed as a drunk. But even though I could see the book with my eyes closed, as soon as I opened them the words vanished. I knew those words were in me, I just had to squeeze them out.

I preferred getting up early in the morning since it was the only time I had the house to myself. I put on my old blue private-school pants which were now too tight because I was having a growth spurt. I yanked a white T-shirt down over my head and slipped into Dad's old mud-stained loafers. Mom had given up on dressing me as a catalogue cover boy for Sears, so I dressed myself to look like a combination mental-health outpatient and day laborer so I'd blend in with the tough local kids. I ran my fingers through my hair as I walked down the hall, past Betsy's room, and into the kitchen. BeauBeau III was sleeping in front of the refrigerator door like some bridge troll trying to collect a fee each time it was opened. I gave him a little kick in the rear. "Come on," I whispered, "time to make the donuts." He hopped up and began to stretch. His fleas stretched. His worms stretched. His ticks stretched. Everything but his brain stretched. He was a mess. I figured if I were a dog I'd be just like him.

I pulled out the carton of milk, flipped open the spout, and held it to my mouth. I loved ice-cold milk and took a long drink, swallowed, and drank some more before I began to gag. I dropped to my knees and spit up a clot of sour milk onto the kitchen floor. It jiggled about like a white cube of coagulated Jell-O. Fortunately, BeauBeau III was hungry, and before I could clean the floor he lapped up what I had spit out. Who's the bigger idiot? I wondered. Me or BeauBeau III? I didn't know the answer just yet, but he was definitely my main competition. We were neck and neck in the Bonehead Sweepstakes.

BeauBeau III was Betsy's new dog. Last year, when we all lived in Barbados, Betsy had decided she was going to go to boarding school in London. When we left the island she stayed behind, packed and ready to go. But her plans didn't work out and she grudgingly returned from Barbados to join us back in Fort Lauderdale. She called Florida "the hairy armpit of the world" and was so depressed Mom let her pick out a pet in an effort to lift her spirits. One afternoon she returned from the Animal Rescue League with an already grown cocker spaniel, and just like BoBo I, who'd been eaten by an alligator in a canal near our old house in Fort Lauderdale, and BoBo II, who we had to leave behind in Barbados, and BoBo-the-Chihuahua, who'd been flattened by a car, this one had no trace of a brain. Betsy was now studying French and she had named him BeauBeau III. The prissy French name didn't make him any smarter. Betsy could educate his palate with all the French food she wanted—French bread, French fries, French toast, and French dip—she could dress him up in a beret, knot a scarf around his neck, and spray him with French perfume, yet he'd still be nothing more than a common American BoBo who cuts loose with paralyzing nerve gas during dinner, pees down his own leg when excited, eats palmetto bugs, and laps up Eric's baby vomit. But I loved him. He was my soul mate, my double, and was fast becoming my mentor. I was dumb and miserable, and I looked to him to teach me how to be dumb and happy. So far, I wasn't doing too well.

As I ran a sponge over the sticky spot on the floor, BeauBeau licked at my hand. His breath almost blistered my skin. "You're revolting," I said, turning my nose away from him. "Go outside and dig a hole."

He didn't need my permission. He squeezed his way through the cat-size rubber pet-door and into the backyard. Digging holes was his obsession. He had dug so many our yard looked like a World War I battlefield. And he dug the deepest holes of any dog I'd ever seen. He could work his entire body below the surface and as he tunneled toward the center of the earth the dirt sprayed up and formed a mound to one side. In his former life he must have been a grave robber who'd been punished when he died by being reincarnated as a dumb dog.

I brushed my teeth, washed my face, and, since I was already dressed, sprayed deodorant on the outside of my shirt. I grabbed my black book from the bedroom floor and shoved it into my backpack. I carried it with me at all times just in case my muse decided to pay a visit while I was on the bus, or trying to figure out how to open my combination lock at school. A muse could strike at any time, the old writers' magazine had stressed, "even while one was engaged in personal hygiene." I wanted to be prepared.

I had just slung the backpack over my shoulder and was tiptoeing down the hallway when Betsy cracked open her bedroom door.

"Have a nice day, BeauBeau the fourth," she sang. She had been calling me that ever since I announced the results of my school aptitude tests at the dinner table. That was a colossal mistake. Telling my family that I was dumb was even more proof that I really was dumb. If I was even a little bit smart, I would have kept my mouth shut.

I faked a lunge at Betsy and growled. I had already pulled the pins out of her door hinges—my favorite trick—and was praying she might yank the door open a little farther so it would fall back and flatten her. But she held her ground and glared at me.

"Make sure your address is sewn inside your pocket in case you get lost," Betsy advised.

I wanted to scream out, "I'm not an idiot! Leave me alone!" But if I woke the baby Mom would get involved in a bad way. So I just sucked it up, took a deep breath, and thought I'd sew some other family's address labels on me, get lost, and be sent to a home full of nice people. And I'd take BeauBeau III with me, too.

Even when my family was trying to be thoughtful toward me, it hurt. The day before, I'd found a package of alphabet flash cards that Pete hid in my backpack. After I got him in a headlock and had BeauBeau lick his face, he said he was just trying to help educate me. And for the last two weeks Mom cooked me fish sticks for dinner because she said fish was "brain food."

Dad was the only one who didn't seem to mind that I was dumb. He said that if I was going to work with my hands for the rest of my life brains would just get in the way. He had taken a new job at a concrete factory and said I could always work in the warehouse as the rat exterminator. "You just take a broom handle and pound a rusty nail through the end. And when you see a rat chewing a bag of 'crete you just stab him through the brain." The thought of rat juice squirting out of a punctured brain gave me nightmares.

I continued down the hall and slipped out the front door before anyone else woke up and gave me a hard time. As I walked down the sidewalk toward the bus stop, BeauBeau was already deep into a hole. I could just see his tail wagging and a fan of dirt overhead.

"Go, BeauBeau, go," I hollered. "Dig a hole to France and we'll visit your relatives." He hopped out of the hole and shook the dirt from his coat. I peeled the wrapper off a Slim Jim I had saved for lunch, took a bite, and threw the rest in his direction. He snapped it out of the air and swallowed it whole. "See you later, buddy," I said. He barked and went back to work.

Two

I began to call myself insulting loser names shortly after I was sent to Sunrise Junior High. It was known as a tough school, full of kids with low potential and no plans for the future. Gary Pagoda had gone there until he failed three years in a row and dropped out. He had already been a veteran juvenile delinquent by seventh grade, and even *he* swore it was dangerous. He called it a school for the "criminally insane." So I had figured it was like a prison filled with hardened convicts with swastikas tattooed onto their foreheads and homemade knives strapped inside their motorcycle boots. That was only a guess.

What really shocked me was when I found out how true my guess had been. After I had been at Sunrise for a few weeks I'd heard all about the school's peculiar history. Before it was a school, Sunrise Junior High had been Sunrise State Detention Center. When Florida still had chain gangs working to pick up trash and cut weeds on the side of highways, the criminals had been housed in the same rooms where I now studied English, math, science, and wood shop.

This made a lot of sense when I looked at the school's architecture. The double rows of twenty-foot-high chain-link fences were topped with rusty barbed wire that over the years had snagged a lot of plastic grocery bags. When the wind picked up, the bags snapped back and forth and sounded just like the tough girls smacking their gum as they lined up outside the phone booth. There were steel gates that led into the school, two in the front and two in the back. The stone towers sticking up at every corner had been guard shacks where trained snipers could pick off any escapees. Now one tower was used as a science and weather station, another as a "Time Out" zone for hyperactive bullies, one as the DARE office, and the other as headquarters for the Latin Club. I guessed they were the only club that got a tower because the few token smart kids needed to barricade themselves in from the illiterate Huns all day.

The more I poked around the school, the more evidence I found of the old prison. About every fifty feet down each corridor, there were swinging metal doors with bullet-proof glass panels. Broken security cameras mounted on steel poles were everywhere, inside and outside. There were thick bars over all the classroom windows. But the strangest thing about Sunrise was the wood and sheet-metal machine shop where prisoners had made institutional furniture, license plates, military dog tags, and other stuff no one else would make unless they were in prison. It was the size of a football stadium. This was why Sunrise was a magnet school for vocational training in *shop*. Kids—mostly guys—from all over Fort Lauderdale were bused to our school just to make benches, picture frames, jewelry boxes, letter openers, salad sets, bedside tables, baseball bats, and other stuff they sold in a little gift store next to the Department of Social Services office, which was next to the principal's office.

There was only one way to escape from Sunrise aside from tunneling under the fences. You had to *test* your way out of the school. You had to *prove* you were smart enough to be sent to a magnet school for the arts or sciences, or a school with a college-preparatory curriculum. And so I had signed up for the tests, figuring I'd be transferred out of there in no time.

Mr. Ploof was the Guidance Counselor. One Monday, as arranged, I went into his small office, which had probably been a padded isolation cell. He had prepared a battery of tests for me.

"Are you ready to exercise your mental muscle?" he asked, and pointed to his own hydrocephalic cranium, which was as hairless and white as the belly on a watermelon.

"I can't wait," I replied. "I've been thinking about this all night long."

"Should have just got some sleep," he remarked. "'Cause you're in for a long day."

He started out by timing how fast I could stack a hundred small washers onto a thin metal rod. I didn't even turn my brain on for that one. Instead, I daydreamed about my future. I figured in about a week I'd be in a school where the teachers actually helped students to write books. All day we'd read stacks of great novels and discuss them inside and out until we knew everything about how they were written. Then we'd write and rewrite our own books until we sent them off to be published.

Afterward Mr. Ploof gave me a tray of fifty assorted nuts and bolts and I had to fit the proper nuts to the proper bolts as quickly as possible. It was a breeze.

"Pretty good manual dexterity," Mr. Ploof remarked, nodding as he jotted down some figures on a pad.

"I write a lot," I said, stretching the truth. "Keeps the fingers limber. Besides, our dog can do this stuff."

"Don't go getting a swelled noggin," he warned, as his monstrous head wobbled dangerously on his skinny neck. "The tests get harder."

"Just bring it on," I said, feeling supremely confident that I was soon going to have my ticket out of this loser school.

I did a test where I read a page of mixed-up information, then summarized it in the most logical order. That took only an ounce of common sense. Then I had a long list of sentences where I filled in the blanks about my *feelings*. That took me extra time to sort through because I always felt two or three ways about any one thing that happened to me.

After that test I was a bit run down and asked if I could take a break, stretch my legs, and eat a snack. I had a family-size Zero bar stashed in my locker.

"No," he replied. I had begun to figure out that he was one of those people who stressed every word with a gesture. He said no while at the same time slowly rotating his head back and forth. A double no. Even if you didn't understand English, you would get the universal sign language for no.

"You have to do this all in a row," he explained. "Plus, you can't be left alone. How can I tell you won't *cheat*?" To illustrate that he had asked a question his hands darted out from his sides like a puzzled Egyptian hieroglyphic.

"How can I cheat?" I asked. "The questions are a secret. Besides, you can come with me."

"Pull yourself together," he said, and narrowed his eyes. "Part of this test is endurance." He jutted out his chin, but his head began to tilt forward so he pulled it back. Then he removed the standard IQ test from its sealed envelope and placed it face-down in front of me. "Now I want you to concentrate," he instructed, and tapped a finger against his temple. "Of everything you've done today, this is the most important. The IQ results will go on your permanent record and will be with you for the rest of your life."

It was as if he was reading me my Miranda rights—*you have the right to remain silent, the right to call an attorney, the right to . . .*

He removed a stopwatch from his pocket. "On your mark. Get set." He pressed the top button. "Go!" he shouted, and pointed toward an imaginary finish line.

I was so revved up I put too much pressure on my pencil and as I wrote down the first answer my point snapped. I desperately looked up at Mr. Ploof. "Can I start over?" I asked.

He frowned down at me. "No talking. Keep going!" he instructed.

I didn't have a pencil sharpener so I began to gnaw at the wood around the lead, spitting out the pulp, until I exposed the blunt end. I felt even more like a white laboratory rat, but I pulled myself together and raced through the test. For something so important it didn't seem too difficult or take very long even though I got off to a rough start. I found it more challenging when Mom asked me to sort the laundry into lights and darks and I had to decide where to put clothes that were mauve or salmon or chartreuse. But I never thought that sorting the laundry was an indication of my future potential.

When I lowered my pencil Mr. Ploof pressed another button on the stopwatch and wrote the time down on his pad.

"You can go now, but return next week for the results," he said.

"Thanks," I replied, picking at a few splinters in my lips. I dashed out the door and down the hall. I was starving, so I got my Zero bar from my locker and went into the boys' toilet. There were a couple of scrawny guys in there smoking cigarettes and taking turns punching each other so hard in the chest that twin plumes of dragon smoke rolled out their noses. I swallowed my Zero bar too quickly and it got stuck in my throat.

A week later I was back in Mr. Ploof's office.

"Sit down," he said, and pointed to a ruggedly carved chair that was probably made by a former ax murderer. Then he patted the seat of his own matching chair so I wouldn't misunderstand him. "Take a load off."

"I'd rather stand," I said. I was pretty nervous so I jumped to the point. "What about the test results? Can I go to another school?"

He sat down and sighed. "Sorry, kid," he said, trying to sound cheerful as he opened my file. "You're just normal. Average."

"That can't be," I protested. "Just earlier this year I was better than average. In fact, I was *superior.*"

He rolled his eyes. "You may have peaked early," he suggested. "It happens." He spun my file around so I could read it for myself. "You didn't show us any reason to send you up to the next level."

I sat down. Typed out on a sheet of paper were my test results.

PHYSICAL DEXTERITY—AVERAGE

LOGIC SKILLS—AVERAGE

EMOTIONAL MATURITY—AVERAGE

IQ—LOW TO AVERAGE—85

"I don't have a low IQ," I said with my voice rising. "No way I'm this—"

He cut me off. "Be grateful it's still in the *average* zone," he stressed. "Believe me, I've seen a lot worse. If anything, this score means you should make something really spectacular in wood shop. Just so you know, before you pitch a fit and insult me, my IQ is also eighty-five." He gave himself a little congratulatory pat on the back.

I was horrified. He was the pinnacle of what I might become. This couldn't be true. It was a nightmare. I stood up and shuffled toward the door. I felt as though I had just received the worst possible sentence: Simpleton for Life Without Parole.

"Don't take it so hard," he advised, and waved at the air in front of his face. "It's not like we're going to send you to Siberia. Just join the crowd. Average guys like you and me are the majority. We're the men that make the world go around. We work in the trenches, digging ditches, unclogging toilets, mowing lawns—you know, the jobs that nobody wants to do but that *have* to be done. Who do rich people call when they need help? Guys like you and me, that's who."

"But I want to be a writer," I said quietly.

"Hey, a low IQ doesn't stop you from writing. You can do phone messages. Grocery lists. Sweetheart tattoos. Graffiti. Heck, you can pass notes back and forth in class, can't you?"

"But I want to write books," I explained.

He scratched his hairless head. "That," he replied, "could prove to be frustrating. Why defeat yourself by trying to become something you can't?"

"But I can try," I said. "Whatever happened to the idea that if at first you don't succeed, try, try again?"

"I guess nobody told you," he said matter-of-factly. "That little ditty is for losers, for old dreamers like me," and he pointed to his huge cranium, "who beat their head against the wall one too many times. Look, do yourself a favor. Pick something you can handle."

"Like a broom?"

"Now you're thinking," he said with fresh enthusiasm. "Now you're putting those brain cells to work."

"Thanks," I said in a whisper, and backed out of his office. I stumbled down to the boys' toilet and splashed water on my face. I wished those guys were in there punching each other. I would have asked them to put me out of my misery like a horse with a broken leg.

Three

When I got off the school bus I went straight to the library. I always had a few extra minutes before wood shop started and figured the library was the most logical location for my muse to take some quiet time and visit me.

But the library was such a non-creative place it made sense that my muse never showed up. First, the few books we had were tethered on loops of braided wire to screw hooks on the shelf, just like telephone books wired to U-bolts in telephone booths. And second, we didn't have a librarian. We had a volunteer dad. He was a retired bank security guard who had been shot in the knee during an armed robbery. He ambled around with one leg pulling up the rear as if he were dragging a ball and chain. I guessed wiring the books to the shelves was his way of making sure they weren't stolen, but the result was more of a prison for books.

The first time I went to the library I asked him how I checked one out.

"This isn't a lending library," he replied. "It's a sit and read library." He pointed to one of the long locker-room-type benches running along all the shelves.

"But I can't sit here and read all day," I said.

"Then don't read so much," he suggested. "Stay busy doing other things. Besides, it's unhealthy for a young man to be cooped up in a library all day."

I changed the subject. "Do you have any books on writing?" I asked. "Such as how-to books on novels or stories? How to get in touch with your muse?"

"Kid," he said wearily, "the best how-to advice I can give you is if you want to do something, do it. Don't sit around reading about it. You want to write? Then go write. Now, why don't you take a hike. Don't you see I'm busy?"

He turned away from me and began to drill a hole through the top corner of a book so he could fit a wire through and secure it to a shelf.

"Is that a new book?" I asked.

He didn't answer. He just turned up the drill speed. Bits of paper spiraled out of the hole. I could make out a few letters where he'd drilled through a word. I hoped it wasn't a how-to book on something like first-aid. Instead of giving someone the Heimlich, you'd give them a hernia. When I didn't leave right away he looked at me and jerked his head toward the door. I wasn't that dumb. I turned and left.

This time, when I entered the library, the volunteer dad was tightening nuts on the underside of the shelves, securing his screw hooks, and examining the wire cables to make sure they were undamaged.

He turned toward me and eyed me up and down. "I've been looking for you," he said. "Come here."

"Did you get any new books on how to write novels?" I asked.

"No," he growled. Then quickly he grabbed me by the shoulders and pushed me up against a book shelf. "Stand with your arms overhead and your feet apart," he ordered as he swooped around me.

"What's this all about?" I asked.

"I'm going to search you," he explained. "Someone's been coming in here with a wrench and wire cutters and stealing my books." He patted me down from the tips of my fingers to my toes. Then he unzipped my backpack and shook everything out onto a table. "Where're you hiding them?" he asked.

"I don't know what you're talking about," I replied.

"The books!" he snapped. "The books you stole."

"I don't steal books," I said. "I borrow them."

"That's what they all say," he snarled, clearly disappointed that I wasn't the thief. "Don't you have a class to go to?"

"Yes," I said.

"Then get," he ordered.

As I left the library I looked up at the ceiling one last

time just in case my muse was getting ready to visit. Nothing was up there but a big rusty stain.

On Monday and Tuesday we had English, math, science, and history, as did any other normal school. But on Wednesday, Thursday, and Friday we did nothing but *shop*. We didn't have gym because the principal figured exercise was a waste of time for guys who were just going to grow up, do manual labor, maybe play a little softball, and retire to drink beer. Because I had gone to school in Barbados for most of seventh grade, I had missed all the metal-shop instruction and was now into the final weeks of wood shop before school ended.

After I fled the library I went down to the shop and, along with fifty other guys, stood in front of my assigned piece of heavy equipment.

"Today, men, we're going to work at making baseball bats," announced Mr. Gilette, the wood-shop instructor. He wore tan bib overalls and a hardware-store paint cap. "The bat is one of man's earliest and most essential tools, which makes it the perfect assignment for learning to operate a wood lathe."

Great, I thought, then we can beat each other's brains out during recess. Those who survive can then evolve and make spears. The next round of survivors can make bows and arrows. The winner and sole survivor can build a mahogany trophy case with the heads of all his victims on display as an example of his superior evolution.

"Each one of you should have a four-inch by four-inch by four-foot piece of pine already inserted in your lathe."

We did.

"Now, to quote Michelangelo, the secret to carving a really good bat is visualizing the finished object within the raw materials."

I raised my hand.

"Yes," said Mr. Gilette.

"I don't think Michelangelo sculpted baseball bats," I ventured.

"What's your name, young man?" he asked.

"Jack Henry," I replied.

He made a note in his green roll book. "Well, Mr. Henry," he said, and marched forward to tower over me. "Michelangelo, among other things, invented baseball bats."

"I was always under the impression it was Fred Flintstone," I said, wondering what other smart-ass things I could say in order to get kicked out of shop.

"No. It was definitely Michelangelo," he insisted.

"Are you sure David and Goliath weren't the first pitcher-batter combo?" I asked, still hoping to get the boot.

A few guys began to laugh.

"Michelangelo," Mr. Gilette persisted, then snapped his fingers overhead to cut off the laughter. "Now back to what I was saying." He spoke as if he were pounding a sixteen-penny nail through my skull. "Imagine, if you will, that Babe Ruth has come to you with the request to make him a bat for the seventh game of the World Series. A perfect bat. A homerun-hitting monster bat. Now, let that be your inspiration as we begin to *visualize*. First, put on your protective goggles."

We did. I visualized us all as annoying houseflies.

"Next, start your lathes by flipping up the toggle switch on the lower right."

We did and the sound of the fifty electric motors picking up speed was like a jet screaming toward takeoff.

"Now," he hollered above the roar. "Take your wood chisel and begin to press the sharp edge against the handle end of the bat, and don't be afraid to bear down on the wood and let the chips fall where they may."

I pressed the chisel against the rotating four-by-four. A corner of the blade dug into the wood and in an instant the chisel was whipped out of my hand and sent hurtling end-over-end toward the front of the shop, where it hit the brick wall and clattered onto the floor next to Mr. Gilette's steel-toed work boot.

"Cut! Cut!" Mr. Gilette shouted, but most everyone was bearing down on their bats. Long ribbons of yellow pine curled up over their heads as they dreamed of the perfect club for "the Babe." Mr. Gilette tripped a master circuit breaker and killed all the power. The lathes slowly wound down.

"What are you, Henry?" Mr. Gilette shouted directly into my face. "Brain dead? Or just limp-wristed?"

"I slipped," I explained.

"Have you tested high enough to be in shop?" he asked.

"I'm warm-blooded," I replied. It was beginning to dawn on me that if I was a big enough jerk they might do me a favor and suspend me indefinitely. A lot of writers got their start by being thrown out of school.

He picked up the chisel, then turned and slapped it handle first into my open hand. "If this thing had hit me just right, mister, I'd be dead and you'd be up on manslaughter charges."

"And I'd be convicted and sent right back to this school," I retorted.

He hastily removed a pad of pink slips from his nail apron. He wrote down: *Jack Henry. One hour extra shop for mouthing off.* He kept a copy for the principal and folded the other in half and shoved it down into my shirt pocket. "See you after school, motor-mouth," he said.

No you won't, I thought as I returned to my lathe.

"Let us once again imagine the unformed object within the wood," announced Mr. Gilette and switched the circuit breaker back on. The lights dimmed and flickered as if someone were being put to death in the electric chair.

By the time I finished, my bat looked more like a walking stick for a blind man. Babe Ruth could only have used it to tap his way around the bases.

At lunchtime I marched over to the cafeteria to get something to eat. Creamed chicken gizzards was the main course of the day. It had been the main course on Wednesdays since I got to the place. The cafeteria boss only allowed us plastic spoons to eat with. I guess she figured plastic knives and forks were too dangerous for us criminals in training. The slippery gizzards were pretty hard to manage with just a spoon. As I walked down a row of steel tables someone put pressure on a gizzard and it shot off the tray and onto the waxed concrete floor, where it skidded away like an escapee slug. I dodged a few more and bought a carton of milk from a tough-looking kitchen lady with a mustache. I figured she was some Mafia guy hiding in the Witness Protection Program.

I took the milk and went out to the ex-prison yard to pace back and forth and figure out a way to blow off detention. I needed an excuse to be someplace else. I thought of going to visit Mr. Ploof for more career counseling, but that was too depressing. I couldn't volunteer at the library because the library dad thought I was a book thief. Then I saw the sign on one of the guard towers. LATIN CLUB MEETING AFTER SCHOOL. ALL INVITED. I decided to check them out.

At the end of shop I raised my hand and asked Mr. Gilette if I could go to the bathroom.

"The old bathroom trick before detention," he said. "Do you think I'm going to fall for that?"

"Really," I said. "I have to go."

"I'll give you a two-minute head start," he said with a knowing smile. "Then when I find you, which I will, I'm going to teach you how to make toothpicks."

I used my two minutes to dash across the prison

grounds and over to the Latin Club tower. It will be nice to hang around with some smart kids for a change, I thought, as I pounded on the metal door.

A peek window slid open and a voice called out in Latin, *"Quis ibi est?"*

"Jack Henry," I replied, guessing that my name was the most logical answer. For about ten seconds I heard my name whispered back and forth. I looked over my shoulder. I didn't see Mr. Gilette.

"What do you want?" asked another voice, this time in English.

"I want to join your club," I said. "Hurry."

"You have to know some Latin," he replied.

"E pluribus unum," I blurted out. *"Semper fi. Carpe diem."* That was all I could think of and it was as good as admitting I was a *dim bulb, non-Latin-speaking loser.* I didn't even know pig-Latin.

They swung open the door, grabbed me by the arm, and yanked me inside. As soon as I was clear of the doorway they slammed the door and lowered a wooden barricade.

It was dark and when my eyes adjusted to the candlelight I realized I was in a room with something like a handful of Shermans from the Rocky and Bullwinkle show.

"Thanks," I said.

"If you want to be a member you have to pass a Latin test," one boy said, eyeing me suspiciously. He handed me a sheet of paper and a pencil and pointed to a desk.

"Can I take this home with me?" I asked. "I don't test well under pressure."

"No," he insisted. "Now start."

I stared down at the paper. I couldn't even understand the directions. It was a fill-in-the-blanks Latin test so I knew immediately I was sunk. Here we go again, I thought. I could just picture Mr. Ploof saying, "Don't worry, kid, you'll make something really spectacular in wood shop."

"Look," I said, "I'll be honest with you. I don't know Latin. But I'm a smart kid and I'm hiding from the shop teacher, and I promise to learn it if you just let me hide out here."

"You take shop?" the president said with disgust. "That automatically disqualifies you. Nobody in the Latin club takes shop."

"Your sign said all-invited," I reminded him.

"Read between the lines," one of the Shermans shot back. "All *smart* kids invited. Not some woodblock."

"Some woodchip," said another.

"Woodpile," added a third.

"Woodrot." The fourth member opened the door and I stepped out into Mr. Gilette's shadow.

"Don't worry, kid," he said, and grabbed the collar of my shirt. "Everyone tries to escape to the Latin Club at least once while they're at Sunrise. Now come on back to the shop and I'll show you a trick on how to stack a thousand perfect toothpicks into one tiny box."

There is just no place for me here, I thought, as Mr.

Gilette steered me forward. I'm not a shop jock, or some Latin nerd, but somewhere in between. According to the old writers' magazine I read, all writers are misfits who have to make their own private place in the world. I had no idea where that private place might be, but I desperately wanted to find it.

Four

When I finally returned home from school after detention BeauBeau was waiting for me. He had been busy all day digging holes and as I walked up the street he ran circles around the house barking and springing through the air with dumb doggy joy. Maybe he didn't have a brain, but he was having a great life.

"Be right with you," I called to him. After I changed into my work clothes I went outside through the sliding glass door and picked up my shovel. According to Mr. Ploof it was the perfect tool for me. I'd never have to work with a pen, a scalpel, a telephone, a firehose, or anything that took some brains to operate. For me it was just a good old-fashioned back-breaking round-faced shovel.

Since BeauBeau was Betsy's dog she was responsible for his deranged behavior. But she didn't want to fill in the holes he dug so she was paying me a nickel for each hole filled. It wasn't a lot of money, but it was steady work. BeauBeau and I were a team. All day he'd dig 'em, and when I returned from school I'd fill 'em. It was the kind of assembly-line work that Mr. Ploof had suggested.

One of the main differences I could find between myself and BeauBeau was that after he finished a hole he was so excited he ran about ten circles around the house. He barked and announced to all the other dogs in the neighborhood, "Hey, I dug a hole. Look at me. I dug a hole. I'm great. Hey! Come see the hole I dug." Then after he calmed down he'd dig another hole right next to the old hole. On the other hand, once I filled in a hole I'd just add one more nickel to the total, take a self-pitying deep breath, and start filling in another. I had nothing to cheer about, and that is what tipped me off that something was wrong. If I was so dumb, then why was I so unhappy? It was because the tests were wrong. If I was as dumb as they said, then I'd be like BeauBeau. Each time I'd fill in a hole I'd run around the house, waving my shovel overhead and shouting with mindless joy. But filling holes was boring, dumb, brainless work and it was a waste of my time. I didn't need to be a genius to know that.

I threw down my shovel, dropped onto one knee, and looked up into the air with my eyes closed. "Come on, muse," I whispered, "I need you now more than ever. Give me some novel-writing inspiration. I'm ready. I'm waiting. And I'm willing."

I bowed my head and waited for fresh words to flood my brain. But it was a repeat of what I'd heard before.

Idiot. Moron. What makes you think you can write a novel? I quickly hopped up and walked off the sting of those words. With each step I was beginning to smarten up. This muse business can't be right, I thought, as I paced back and forth. Only an idiot like me would believe that a muse might come down from the sky and whisper brilliant words into my ear.

I looked at BeauBeau. He was in a hole digging as if he had found a dinosaur bone. He may have had a dog-sized brain but he was smart enough to know exactly what he liked to do. He wasn't waiting for a dog muse to tell him to dig holes.

I didn't have to be real bright to know that if I wanted to accomplish anything I shouldn't magically expect it to just happen. Waiting for a muse was like begging for a handout, or looking for a free ride. Writing was probably nothing more than plain old hard work. And that's why more people didn't write. They took the easy way out and dug holes.

"BeauBeau, you're too dumb to know it but you're a genius. Now, hurry up and dig," I said, spurring him on. "A few more nickels and we can go to the public library for a good book on writing, and a Slim Jim."

The promise of a Slim Jim really got him going, and in ten minutes he had a huge hole so long and wide he could turn around in it without hitting the sides.

"Good dog," I cheered. "You just made me another nickel. In fact, that is a two-nickel double-thick Slim Jim crater."

He jumped out of the hole and was thrilled. He ran around me barking wildly, throwing his head back and yapping with abandon. The pre–Slim Jim saliva ran down the sides of his mouth. He stood up and pranced around his hole on his hind legs with his front paws paddling the air.

"Go, BeauBeau, go," I shouted. "Do that hole-diggin' dance."

He barked, then tore off running around the house, and with each circle he picked up speed like a tornado.

"Faster," I hollered and waved him forward. "Faster." His ears pressed back against his head. His tongue stuck out. He kicked up dirt as he sprinted past me, then turned the corner and was out of sight. But in a moment he reappeared around the far corner.

"Do it, BeauBeau. Go for the Slim Jim gold!" I shouted.

He must have gotten a little dizzy from circling the house because he began to stumble as he adjusted his balance. Then he lost his equilibrium altogether and darted full speed off to one side and plunged head-first into his double-sized hole. I heard an awful snap, and a yelp, and that was all.

I threw down my shovel and ran over to him. His head was bent back against his shoulder. "BeauBeau!" I hollered, and grabbed him under his belly and lifted him out. I laid him out on his side and straightened out his head. Somehow I knew he was dead, but I couldn't believe it. Maybe he was just unconscious.

I ran into the house and pounded on Betsy's closed

door. "BeauBeau fell into a hole and I think he broke his neck," I blurted out all in one breath.

"He's French," she replied from the other side. "They faint if they have an ingrown toenail. Just tell him the Germans are invading and he'll jump up and start running."

"He's not acting," I cried. "He busted his neck. I heard it snap."

Suddenly she whipped her door open real fast and as I yelled, "Look out," it flew off its hinges and crashed to the floor.

"You are worse than stupid," she said angrily and punched me in the chest, knocking the wind out of me. "You're criminal."

She ran down the hall and out the back door.

I fought to catch my breath as I crawled down to the kitchen and grabbed a bottle of ammonia from under the sink. I unscrewed the cap and took a deep whiff and my breath came roaring right back. Good stuff, I thought. If he was just unconscious, then this would bring him around.

When I caught up to Betsy she was kneeling by BeauBeau's side with her ear pressed against his chest. Pete was leaning over her and Dad was coming around the corner. After a minute Betsy said, "No heartbeat." She held his neck just under his jaw. "No pulse. We better get him to the vet."

I threw the ammonia to one side and the plastic bottle hit Pete in the head. He fell in the hole. I thought he might have broken his neck but I didn't have time to do anything about it. BeauBeau was my main concern.

Betsy grabbed BeauBeau's chest and I grabbed his rear, and we carried him to the car.

"Don't put him on the seat," Dad hollered. "Put him over the front fender, like a deer. When you croak your bladder lets loose."

"Thanks for the real-life detail," Betsy snapped. "But we're trying to save a life here."

We lifted BeauBeau into the trunk. I climbed in and curled up next to him, then quickly ducked as Betsy slammed down the top.

Dad seemed to hit every bump, and I kept saying, "Don't worry. I'll take care of you. If you live, you can have a Slim Jim as long as the Alaska pipeline." I patted him on the neck, but then jerked my hand back. "Sorry," I said.

After Dad parked he unlocked the trunk. I hopped out and we hustled BeauBeau into the pet emergency room and laid him out on a metal table.

"He's definitely dead," the vet declared. He swung BeauBeau's head back and forth as if it were a rag doll's. "Broken neck."

Betsy sighed dramatically. "It's always the brilliant ones that die young," she said, then pointed to me. "That's why you'll live forever."

I turned away from her because I could feel the tears well up in my eyes, and I wasn't ready to fight back. I put a hand on BeauBeau's side. "Sorry, buddy," I said. "I won't forget you. I promise. You were an inspiration to me."

"What do you want me to do with him?" the vet asked.

"Whatever you do to the rest," Dad replied. "As long as it's free."

"Cremation," the vet replied.

"Can we get the ashes?" I asked. I could keep them in my piggy bank.

"Sorry," he said. "They all get mixed together—cats, dogs, squirrels, weasels, whatever."

On the way back to the car I was struck with an idea. At first I thought my muse had finally woke up, but then I realized it was just a brilliant idea that I had thought of on my own. I turned and went back into the vet's office. His assistant was struggling to slide BeauBeau into a plastic trash bag. The poor guy had already begun to stiffen up.

"Can you just freeze him?" I asked her. "You know, keep him on ice until I scrape up some money for a proper burial?"

I didn't know what a proper burial meant for a dog, but it sounded respectful.

"Sure," the nurse said. "We can keep him for a week."

"Thanks," I replied.

I went back to the car.

"What was that all about?" Dad asked.

"A private goodbye," I said. If I told him what else was on my mind he'd give *me* a proper burial.

Five

The next day, as Mr. Gilette called roll, everyone announced what he was going to make for his final woodshop project. Mr. Gilette had been instructing us for weeks to come up with something "brilliant and useful," but not until BeauBeau died was I inspired with the perfect idea.

"Allston," hollered Mr. Gilette.

"Here," Allston replied. "Gun rack."

"Campbell?"

"Yo. Canoe."

"Henry?"

"Present. Dog coffin."

"Excuse me," Mr. Gilette said, and peered up over his roll book. "Did I hear 'dog coffin'?"

"Yes, sir," I replied.

"A dog coffin is not an acceptable project," he proclaimed. "Dogs don't need coffins. They just need a hole and some dirt." Behind me the class began to laugh.

But I stood my ground and said, "I think a dog deserves as much respect as a person."

"Look," Mr. Gilette explained, "from my point of view most humans don't deserve coffins. And the whole idea of the final project is to make something that you could actually sell. Something that you could start a business with, like gun racks or shoeshine kits, or canoes. But not dog coffins."

"Well, I think it's an exceptional business idea," I continued. "You can only use it once and then you have to buy a new one. It's the American way."

The class cracked up. I could sense they were shifting to my side and that encouraged me. Once I got it out of my mind that I was supposed to be dumb, I actually felt pretty smart.

And then Mr. Gilette did what teachers love to do when they find their power slipping. He polled the class. "Okay, wise guys," he shouted. "How many of you think a dog coffin is about the most stupid business idea ever cooked up? Raise your hand."

The hands went up as if he had pulled a machine gun on them.

I didn't even bother to count.

"Bury that idea, Mr. Henry," he concluded. "And come up with a new project tomorrow."

But I didn't. The next day he asked again, and again I replied, "Dog coffin."

The class went wild.

"If you persist in making that coffin," Mr. Gilette said, "I guarantee that you'll fail this class."

"But I'm making something worthwhile."

"Worthless is more like it," he cracked. "Why don't you just make a nice bookshelf? A pair of crutches?"

"Dog coffin," I said, standing firm.

"Then don't be surprised when you have to repeat seventh grade," he stated.

I didn't take him seriously. Nobody was stupid enough to fail shop. Even me.

For three days Mr. Gilette encouraged me to work on a different project, and each day I worked on my coffin. For once, I enjoyed the work and thought Dad was right when he said that working with your hands was a useful skill.

I hadn't measured BeauBeau, so when I drew out my plans I figured three feet was long enough. I made the coffin a foot high and made two handles, one for the front and one for the back. On the top I carved, To BeauBeau III, My Inspiration. At the end of the week I carried it home on the bus.

On Saturday morning I went down to Kmart and bought two yards of red satin.

"Taffeta," the sales lady said as she snipped it off the bolt. "Good for prom gowns. What are you going to do with it?"

"Line my dead dog's coffin," I replied.

She didn't say another word, even though I paid her one nickel at a time, which took half an hour.

When I got home I glued the middle of the taffeta to the bottom of the coffin and let the rest of the fabric drape over the sides.

When I was ready Dad took me to the vet's office to retrieve BeauBeau. We carried him out to the car in his plastic bag.

"You sure you want to go through with this?" Dad asked, as he closed the trunk.

"Of course," I replied. "I think it's about the smartest thing I've ever done."

"Well, considering your IQ," he said, "I guess this is pretty good for you. I only wish you would do this at night so the neighbors won't watch."

"Let 'em," I said. "They might learn something about being nice."

But I was glad Dad and the neighbors didn't watch what awful thing I had to do in order to prepare BeauBeau for his final resting place. Once we returned home Dad helped me carry BeauBeau into the garage. Then he left. Pete was with me when I picked BeauBeau up and tried to place him into the coffin. He didn't fit. BeauBeau had seized up solid, and frozen with his legs sticking straight out. When I put him sideways into the coffin his legs made him too wide, and when I turned him onto his back his legs stuck straight up and I couldn't lower the top. I grabbed him by the paws and tried to bend his joints but they wouldn't move. He was as stiff as an iron fence.

"There's only one thing to do," I said to Pete. I could feel the little hairs sticking up all over my body.

Pete read my mind. "No," he shouted.

"Yes!" I insisted. "Get me the three-pound hammer."

"You'll burn in you-know-where for this," he said with his face all twisted up.

"The hammer," I ordered. "Or I'll fit you in here with him."

He dragged the hammer over, then looked away and covered his eyes.

"You'd be better off plugging your ears," I advised him, took aim, and lowered the hammer with both hands. There was an awful crunching noise as I smashed BeauBeau's left front knee. Pete moaned, then started to jump up and down like a pogo stick. I folded that limb over, then hauled off and splintered the right front knee.

"Jack has lost it!" he yelled, and ran off. "He's killing BeauBeau again!"

I knew I had to hurry. If Betsy saw what I was doing she'd turn me in to the Society Against Cruelty to Animals. Who knew what Dad would say? Probably tell me I'd be better off using a band saw.

"Forgive me, BeauBeau," I muttered. I raised the hammer up over my head and brought it down again, and again, until I had busted up all his joints. Then I twisted and snapped his legs back, and tucked them up against his chest. When I finished all the gruesome work I fit him sideways into the coffin and covered him with the taffeta. Sorry, sorry, sorry, I said to BeauBeau. I didn't mean it to be this way.

Hurry, hurry, hurry, I said to myself. I set the coffin top

in place and was pounding the nails in when Mom, Dad, Betsy, and Pete scrambled into the garage. They stared down on me as if I were some serial killer chopping up another victim.

"You're just in time for the funeral," I announced as cheerfully as I could, and drove in the last nail.

"Pete," I ordered, taking control of the situation, "help me pick up the coffin." He grabbed the rear pallbearer handle with both hands. I grabbed the front and we lifted the coffin, then marched solemnly around the side of the house.

"Pick up the pace," Dad said. "The Teeters are looking out their window and I'm sure they think we're burying the baby."

"God forbid," Mom said.

"They probably think we're Satanists," Betsy speculated, and she waved to Mrs. Teeter, who had pulled the picture-window curtain to one side.

Mom made a big sign of the cross so we'd look legitimate. It probably just made us look more ghoulish.

When we arrived at the grave site Pete and I set the casket on the ground.

"Would anyone like to say a few words on BeauBeau's behalf?" I asked, and bowed my head.

Dad began to laugh. "Look," he said dryly, "I liked the dog. But keep in mind that he was so dumb he dug his own grave. What more needs to be said?"

"He barked in French," Betsy added. "So I hope he ends up on the French side of dog heaven."

"With a bunch of French poodles," Pete said.

Mom declined.

"Amen," I croaked, wrapping it up.

Pete and I bent down and lowered the coffin into BeauBeau's double-wide hole. Then I grabbed my shovel and sprinkled a load of dirt on the lid. This is the final hole he dug, I thought, and one of the last holes of his I'll ever fill in. From now on I'm going to be a writer. Not a gravedigger.

Then I made the sign of the cross and said a little prayer.

Betsy was watching me closely. "You should be institutionalized," she proclaimed. "This whole ceremony is the workings of a sick mind."

"I've already been tested," I said proudly. "And I'm not mentally ill."

"He's just really stupid," Pete said. "Leave him alone."

She left in a huff.

I gave Pete a dirty look and pointed to an open hole. "You're next," I said coldly. "You know what I did to BeauBeau. What makes you think I won't do it to you, too?"

He ran.

"Don't turn your back on me," I shouted. "I've already got you sized up for my next wood project. I'm goin' for extra credit!"

Six

Mr. Gilette wasn't fooling.

At dinner Dad unfolded a letter and held it up over his head and waved it around as if he were trying to surrender to the enemy. "You're failing seventh grade," he announced. "It says right here," and he slapped the paper for effect, "that you're getting an F in shop."

"How?" I yelped. "Me. How?"

"Brain dead," Betsy said sadly. "Probably from sniffing too much wood glue."

"Mind yourself," Mom advised. "Jack's not challenged because of glue." She reached across the table and patted me on the head as if I were some drooling cave dweller.

Betsy reconsidered. "You're right," she said. "I'm sorry. It's not glue. He just naturally doesn't have a clue."

I kept looking back and forth at them as they insulted me. This is what BeauBeau must have felt like around this house, I thought. Everyone talking badly about him right in front of his face and all he could do was look at them with big wet doggy eyes.

"You do have a way out," Dad said somberly.

"What?"

"Shop camp," he replied. "Mr. Gilette runs a private woodworking summer camp in Kissimmee. If you attend it's like going to summer school and you'll pass into eighth grade."

"What a racket," I huffed. "What he's doing is criminal. Can't you see what he's up to? He fails me, then he charges us tuition to go to his summer camp."

"Hey," Betsy said, loving every minute of this, "don't blame your problems on someone else. *You* are the nimrod who failed *shop*."

"I have big plans this summer. I'm going to stay home and write a book." I blurted this out. I had no intention of telling anyone. Now I knew they would make even more fun of me. It was bad enough to have told them I was stupid. It was worse to tell them about my dream. "I want to be a writer," I repeated. "Not a whittler."

"Even writers have to pass seventh grade," Betsy started.

"Wait a minute," Dad said, and hushed everyone else who had lined up to take a shot at me. "You want to become a writer? Do you know what the odds are of being a successful writer? It's like becoming a pro basketball player. Millions of kids play, but only a few hundred can be pros. And what do the rest do? They end up spending all their time sitting on the couch watching the game on TV. It's the same with being a writer. What are the odds you'll ever get published? A million to one?"

"That's not the point," I said. But he wasn't listening.

"You might as well sit on your bum all day playing the lottery. No, being a writer is not a career choice. It's a hobby, something you do after work. What you need for a career is a skill, and I think woodworking is a good place to begin. So I don't want to hear any more about it. Besides, I already talked to Gilette and it's settled. He even gave us a discount because of your diminished abilities. So, next month you're going up to the Kissimmee Wood Shop Camp for Boys."

"But I want to write a book!" I said. "Can't you send me to writers' camp?"

"Don't be so lame," Betsy scoffed, and broke into a laugh. "They don't have camp for writers. People who want to write just do it. They don't wait to go to summer camp for scribblers. And they certainly don't sit around in their bathrobes all day staring toward the heavens while sucking on a piece of brain-damaging lead."

I cringed. She must have seen me waiting for my muse. But that muse business was all over with. From now on I planned to write all my ideas in my black book, and not just wait for them to appear on the ceiling. But now that I was going to wood-shop camp, where would I get the time to write? Especially around guys who carried more penknives than pens in their pockets.

I had one more chance of getting out of shop camp.

The next day after school I stayed behind and spoke with Mr. Gilette.

"Don't fail me," I pleaded. "My dream is to be a writer, not a woodworker."

"Dream on," he said. "I checked with Mr. Ploof and he gave me your test scores. Apparently, even woodworking is a stretch for you."

"Really," I insisted. "I want to be a writer and I was planning to write a book this summer. And you know I worked really hard on that coffin."

"I warned you," he said. "I humiliated you in front of the class. I distinctly said I would fail you if you made that coffin."

"I know, but give me a second chance. I think you judged me too harshly." I said this with all the sincerity I could. Then I looked him right in the eyes and added, "Besides, I'm a good kid."

It worked. "Okay," he said reluctantly. "I don't want to, but I'll give you a second chance because I'm a decent guy. Bring the coffin in tomorrow morning and if it's well made I'll think about giving you a break."

I was shocked. "But it's already in the ground," I stammered. "With a dog in it. A dead dog. My dog."

"I can't give you a grade on what I can't examine," he said matter-of-factly. Then he grinned with the total pleasure of knowing what he was about to say. "A man's gotta do what a man's gotta do. No coffin, no grade change. It's your choice."

"Okay," I said, and staggered out of school in a daze just thinking about what I had to do. When I got home I stood before BeauBeau's grave. "I have nothing but respect for you," I said quietly. "But forgive me, I have to pass seventh grade. I hope you'll understand."

That night I got up out of bed, snuck down to the garage, and got a crowbar out of the toolbox. I hoisted my shovel up over my shoulder and tiptoed around to the backyard. I kept saying to myself, You already did worse to him. Just don't dwell on it. Now dig him up, open the coffin, flip BeauBeau into the hole, cover him up, and take the coffin to school. Once you pass, you can dig him up again, put him back into the coffin, and everything will be as it was. Now just shut up, turn off your low-level brain, and dig a hole like a big dumb BeauBeau IV.

I stood on the grave and looked down at the mound of dirt. It was covered with plastic flowers, BeauBeau's dog toys, his water dish, and a little cross I had made out of Slim Jims. I bent down and carefully removed all the decorations.

When I was ready, I took a deep breath and pushed the shovel into the soft ground, then tossed the dirt to one side. I stuck the shovel in again, and again, until I heard a hollow thud. Too bad it wasn't buried treasure. I hit the top of the coffin lid again. At that moment a neighborhood dog barked and I jumped back as though I had stuck my finger in an electrical socket. I let go of my shovel and ran around to the kitchen door and dashed inside.

"I can't . . . do it," I panted, while standing in the dark. "I'd rather . . . fail seventh grade . . . than dig up the dead."

Even though I said that, I knew I didn't mean it. Deeper within me, a stronger voice roared back. "You can't go to wood-shop camp. You'll be carving ships in a bottle for the rest of your life. Now get out there and do what you have to do."

I took a deep breath, narrowed my eyes, and marched across the yard. Other writers had done what I was about to do. Once I had read about the poet Dante Gabriel Rossetti. When his wife died he put a manuscript of unpublished love poems in her hands just before they closed the coffin. No one in the world would ever read them but her spirit, he thought romantically. She was the love of his life. But a while later he wasn't feeling too romantic when he had a hard time writing any more good poems and needed money. So one dark night he went to the cemetery and dug up his wife and pulled the poems out of her bony fingers. While he had the coffin open he also took the jewels she was wearing. He later published the book and probably pawned the jewels until the checks on the new book started rolling in.

"In order to be a writer," I whispered to myself as I picked up the shovel, "you have to be tough. You have to be willing to dig up the dead for your art. I love you, BeauBeau," I said. "But a man has to do what a dog can't."

When I cleared the dirt from the top of the coffin I put down my shovel. I bent over and wiggled my hand through the damp soil until I felt the pallbearer's handle on the front. I got a grip on it and pulled. The coffin wouldn't budge. I crawled on top of it and began to scoop the dirt out around the sides. I looked over at the house to see if any lights had come on. None. So far, so good. If Betsy came out and saw me she'd call the cops and have me sent to the funny farm, where I'd be hanging out with guys who ate flies for fun.

In a few minutes I had the dirt free from around the edges. I grabbed the handle and pulled up. This time the coffin lifted out and I dragged it across the backyard to the side of the house. Already I could smell something bad.

When I had the coffin behind some bushes the most dangerous part was still to come. I had to get the top off without making so much noise that I'd wake everyone in the house. I felt around the edge of the lid until I could detect a slight opening, then I jammed my crowbar into the crack and pressed down. Then the odor of rotting BeauBeau hit me. It was worse than his breath. I could feel my face contorting as if someone were trying to rip it off, and I began to gag. Some of Mom's fish-stick supper came up into my throat. I swallowed it back down, stood up, and tottered far enough away so I could breathe some fresh air. I was this deep in it already, and I had no choice but to finish the job.

I returned to the garage. I took a rag Dad used for

gasoline spills and wrapped it around my face. "No one ever said being a writer was going to be easy," I said to myself as I knotted the rag behind my head and pulled it down just below my eyes. Then I marched back to the coffin.

Fortunately, I hadn't pounded many nails in the top because I had been in such a hurry to get the lid fastened. The gasoline rag only helped a little. I had to stand away from the coffin, take a deep breath, run back, pry up a nail, then run away from the smell and take a deep breath. Then repeat the process. When I had all the nails loose from the top, I dragged the coffin back over to the grave. I turned away, took one deep breath, then did it. I lifted the lid of the coffin, tossed it aside, and rolled BeauBeau into the hole. I peeked down at him. I shouldn't have. He was covered with a million wiggling white worms that shimmered under the moonlight. I turned away, lifted my mask, and swallowed really hard to keep the fish sticks down. I wiped my mouth across the shoulder of my shirt, lowered my mask, took another deep breath, then worked like a fiend shoveling the dirt back over him and redecorating the ground before I ran to the other side of the yard and took another breath.

I had one more thing to do. I ran back, grabbed the coffin by a handle, and dragged it to the garage. I slipped a green garbage bag on either end and taped it up around the middle. Then I yanked the gasoline rag up over my head, threw it in a corner, and snuck back into the house. I had done it. No one would believe it. But then there was only one person who would have to know—Mr. Gilette.

In the morning when I woke up I could smell something sickly sweet and disgusting. Something rotting. It was me. I sniffed my hands. I wasn't rotting, but the smell of dead BeauBeau was stuck on my skin as if it had been glued there. It was in my hair, and rising up from the pile of clothes on the floor. My pillow smelled, my sheets smelled, the air all around me smelled of dead dog.

Once we had thrown some out-of-date raw chicken in the kitchen trash and had forgotten to take the trash out before going away for the weekend. When we came home the house smelled like a dead person. We couldn't breathe. And even though we opened all the windows and aired everything out, the house reeked of rotting meat for a week. It was awful. Mom still says on really humid days she can smell the dead-chicken odor in her clothes.

And now I smelled worse than that. I threw myself out of bed and ran to the bathroom. I turned on the shower as hot as I could stand it and scrubbed my whole body, even my face, with the stiff-bristled back brush.

When I returned to the bedroom Pete was sitting up in bed.

"Oh, man," he moaned with his face wrinkled up as he sniffed the air. "What did you eat last night?"

"Lots of beans," I said, and rubbed my stomach. "I'm sorry."

"You're stupid, and you smell," he said as he rolled over and pulled the covers across his head.

I raised my fist in the air. "You'll die later," I said. "Once

I figure out a way to dispose of your body." Then I dressed as quickly as possible and went back into the bathroom. I sprayed myself from top to bottom with Bay Rum cologne. What powerful cologne did morticians use, I wondered. I'd love to get some.

When I opened the door to the garage the same gamy smell was in the air. It made the inside of my nose sting. There was nothing I could do about it. I put another layer of trash bags around my coffin and then balanced it across the seat of my bike and the handlebars. I walked it to school. If I took the bus, kids would be climbing out the windows to get away from me.

Mr. Gilette must have thought I would never do what he suggested in order to pass shop. When he saw me drag the coffin through the classroom door he seemed pretty shocked. Then when he smelled me he jumped to action.

"Take that outside," he ordered, as he marched toward me with his hand over his nose and mouth.

"Yes, sir," I replied. I took it around back where all the scrap lumber was kept and began to unwrap the tape and pull off the plastic bags.

When he caught up to me he put his hands on his hips and stared down at the coffin. "Did you actually dig up your dead dog?" he asked.

"Yes, sir," I replied. "I didn't have time to make another coffin."

"Is the dog still in there?" he asked.

"No, sir," I replied.

"Well, it smells like he is."

"It's all the worms," I explained. "And maggots."

I thought he was going to throw up so I got right to the point.

"Are you going to pass me?" I asked.

"Yes," he wailed, pulling the neck of his T-shirt up over his nose as he stepped back. "But not because of your woodwork. Because you're a sick puppy and I don't want to have to deal with you again."

I smiled. "Thank you, sir," I replied.

"Now I want you to go home and put your dog back into that coffin and rebury it," he instructed. "I'll write you a pass."

"Okay," I said. "That was my plan, anyway."

I took the long way home. I wanted to make sure everyone was gone by the time I returned. For a moment I was relieved that I wouldn't have to repeat seventh grade, or go to wood-shop camp. But then I began to imagine what it was going to be like digging BeauBeau back up in the light of day. I could make nose plugs out of Kleenex and cologne, and wear sunglasses. I was going to need rubber gloves to grab him. And I didn't think I'd ever eat a Slim Jim again.

Jack's Tattoo Parlor

Abstract Art

Portraits

So I was reading the news-paper and I half to say, life is a lot more interesting then science fiction. a man was walking down the street when another man jumped out of a window and landed on his head. The guy on the ground got a broken back and the jumper walked away. also, a guy lost his ring on the beach and twenty years later he was fishing, caught a fish, cut it open and

Landscape

Gothic

Nature

Modern

PART TWO

The Blind Leading the Blind, or Fish with Feet

found the ring in its guts. Then some guy out went to catch a train to the city one day. His dog followed him to the station. "Wait for me," the man said then got on the train. In the city he had a heart attack and died. The dog waited and waited and [illegible] day for the [illegible] ten years the dog greeted the trains. Everybody in the [illegible] the dog and took care of it and when it died they put up [illegible] of the dog by the tracks: MAN'S BEST FRIEND, it read.

next day: Pete's in trouble again. He found a set of house keys on the street [illegible] claim he wanted to give them back. So he snuck around to everyone's house and tried the locks but he set off an alarm and the police came and called him a thief but I stuck up for him and told the cops Pete was just insane

One

My dad always said that in order to make a hard job easier you needed the proper tools, like having the perfect three-pound hammer for cracking BeauBeau's legs into place. So I went on a search until I found the perfect writing tool. It was an old portable Underwood manual typewriter that sounded like a Gatling gun when I really got it going. It came in a square black carrying case with a built-in lock and key, and I could fit it into the big front basket of my bicycle and take it to the library, or the beach, or any other lucky writing spot. Plus, it made me look like a writer. A real writer. Not a scribbler. Not a dabbler. Not some kid with a writing hobby. But a real professional with a novel in his brain just aching to be written. That was me. All I needed was a good story and I was ready to cash in.

I got the Underwood for a great price at a yard sale. I had been riding my bike down the street when I saw it. I pulled into the driveway of a very tidy house. Everything the lady had for sale—old photographs, pottery, kitchen utensils, and books—was marked with a little orange price tag neatly stuck to it.

"Does this still work?" I asked the lady, and pointed to the machine.

She looked at me and adjusted the black orchid she had pinned onto her hair. "Try it," she said with a sniff, then puckered her nose up as if she smelled something bad.

There was a sheet of paper in the roller and some non-writers who had only played with the typewriter had typed out a lot of misspelled nonsense. But someone had written, MOST PEOPLE ARE NOT FIT TO RUN THEIR OWN LIVES. That statement was so true it stunned me. In one sentence it summed up exactly how I felt about the world. Excellent writing, I decided. I had to read it twice so I could memorize it. Well, I'm not one of those unfit people, I thought as I rolled the paper up to a clean section. I'm taking charge of my life. This is the summer where I leave the kid Jack behind and leapfrog over high school to become Jack the man. Jack the famous writer. Otherwise, I thought gloomily, I'll have to go back to Sunrise Junior Prison Camp for eighth grade.

I spread my fingers over the keys and pounded out my name and title. JACK HENRY, WRITER. The mechanical sound of the clattering keys snapping forward to hammer the paper was a thousand times better to me than any piano music. The typewriter action was smooth beneath my fingers, and I could tell that the machine liked me. I took roll call, tapping out all the letters, numbers, and punctuation marks in a crisp line, shoulder to shoulder, across the page. They were all there, my troops, and I knew if I could position each one of them in the perfect order I would create something awesome, like when you start one of those ten-thousand-piece jigsaw puzzles. First, you find the four corners, then you link together the straight-edged border pieces, and after that you work like a fiend until you've assembled something as monumental as the entire Battle of Gettysburg. I figured a whole book was written in pretty much the same way, piece by piece.

I rubbed my fingertips on the keys, warming them up, and then I bit down on my lip and typed out my favorite writer's motto: A WRITER'S JOB IS TO TURN HIS WORST EXPERIENCES INTO MONEY. I had read it in the latest issue of a writers' magazine at the drugstore, and thought it was by far one of the most important statements ever written. A lot of small things had gone belly-up for me, but I didn't bother writing about my measly problems. I was waiting to write about something really big and bad. Something hugely disastrous, and so disgusting someone would want to pay money to read it. But so far, nothing good and juicy had come my way. Still, I wasn't panicked. The summer had just begun and there was plenty of time for pain and sorrow and *tragedy.*

I typed a silly poem I had memorized in first grade. BILLY BUILT A GUILLOTINE, TRIED IT ON HIS SISTER JEAN. SAID MOTHER WHEN SHE

BROUGHT THE MOP, THESE MESSY GAMES HAVE GOT TO STOP. The keys didn't stick and the ribbon was still full of black ink. The last writer didn't get much work done. I figured he probably had a cushy life without a problem in the world to write about. My heart started to pick up speed. In an instant I knew that if I owned this typewriter I could turn my *worst experiences into money.* I had to have it. Without it, I was like Samson without his hair—a loser.

"So what do you think, young man?" the yard-sale lady asked me.

"It's okay," I called back to her, lifting my hands from the keys and looking uninterested as I checked my fingertips for dirt. "How much?"

She cleared her throat so loudly the birds in the trees flew away. "I believe the tag clearly reads ten dollars," she replied, and sniffed again in my direction. "Do you smell something foul?" she asked.

It was the curse of BeauBeau. No matter how many showers I took, I still smelled like rotting dog.

"Just mothballs," I said, and curled the corner of my lip up at an open hatbox filled with faded bras and panties she was trying to sell.

It was Sunday afternoon. Her yard sale was almost over. She wouldn't want to drag the typewriter back into the garage, and there was no way I would pay ten bucks for anything, not even to ransom Pete from deranged kidnappers.

"Two bucks," I shot back, and tugged a Baggie with

forty nickels from my pants pocket. I shook it up and down so that the jangle of the coins might entice her.

Her eyes bugged out. "Two dollars?"

"Okay," I said calmly. "One dollar."

Her voice went up an octave, and she got all huffy. "Why don't you just steal it?" she screeched. "Just grab it and run."

I disliked people who didn't know the proper way to bargain. Especially yard-sale people who thought every piece of cruddy junk they owned belonged in a museum. She should have said seven dollars. I'd reply three. She'd say six. I'd say four and we'd agree on five. This is the universal approach to agreeing on a price.

"I don't want to steal it," I said to her. "I'm willing to give you fifty cents for it."

She flipped. "Take it!" she shouted, and began to pitch a hissy fit. "Just take it for free, if you're so cheap! But I never want to see you again!"

Free was a pretty good price, so I snapped the case shut, put it in my bike basket, and took off before she realized she was raving and saying things she didn't mean. Perhaps someday she'd find out she had done a good deed by helping a young writer start his career. Maybe then she'd crack a smile. Maybe not.

Once I had the typewriter, I needed some free time to write without someone looking over my shoulder and telling me to wash the car, cut the grass, run down to the 7-Eleven for milk, or help move furniture around the house as if it was giant pieces in a board game. Then at dinner that night, like a wish come true, my parents announced they were going to take a ten-day summer vacation without us.

"Your dad and I just need a little break from the daily grind," Mom explained, as gently as possible, since *we* were the grind.

I glanced at Dad. His lips were sealed, but I could read his mind: You kids are driving me nuts.

I beamed him my own mental message: Ditto to you, too. You can leave tonight. Take off for the whole summer. I'll become a famous writer and by the time you return you'll have to speak to my book agent before you can speak to me. You'll have to offer me a contract before I'll take out the trash, or cut the grass, or ever lift a finger again.

"We've rented a cottage on the Gulf shore. If anything goes wrong we can come right back. We hope you don't mind," Mom continued, as if reading a script.

"But nothing will go wrong," Dad predicted, and arched an eyebrow so high I thought it was going to pole-vault off his face. "Am I right?"

"You are right," we all replied in unison. No event would be disastrous enough that we couldn't survive it on our own. The house could be sucked down into a sinkhole, we could be victims of a chain-saw massacre, the baby could be carried away by an alligator, and we still wouldn't call him.

Mom put Betsy in charge of Eric, and me in charge of

Pete, which meant I owned him. This was going to be great, I thought. But there was a catch.

"Jack," Dad said, as he tapped his cigarette ashes onto his dinner plate. "What is your summer job? I don't want you just sitting around twiddling your thumbs out on the front porch. There are a lot of older boys in the neighborhood, and since you aren't too swift, they could easily lead you astray."

He caught me by surprise. Still, I knew I didn't want to make money by mowing lawns, or washing cars, or being a professional dog-walker like some of the other kids.

"I'm going to write," I said. "Be a writer."

He smirked. "Are you back on that again? Well, they say simpleminded people are really hardheaded," he said, then whistled off a little steam.

Mom gave him *the look,* and he lightened up a bit.

"Okay, while we're away you can play at writing. But when we come back, if you haven't made any money at it, then I'm going to sneak you in to work at the concrete warehouse. You can keep rats from eating holes in the bags. We had a cat, but the rats ganged up and killed it. You'll just have to lie about your age, but that's no big deal. You're smart enough to do that."

"You bet," I said. But I didn't mean it. I was scared to death of rats, but this was one fear I wouldn't have to face. I had a foolproof way to make quick money from writing. I got the idea from watching television. I was flipping through the channels when, suddenly, I saw it. There was a documentary on Mexico and it showed professional letter writers all lined up on chairs with desks and portable typewriters in a town square. People who had never learned to write would come to them and for a price would dictate letters. The writers would add fancy details, and dress the letters up with lots of adjectives. They made love letters more sexy, sad letters more tragic, and totally humdrum lives worth reading about.

I figured I could do something just like it on Fort Lauderdale beach. I had already gone down to the Salvation Army and bought a stack of old postcards for cheap. At the post office, I tried to bargain for stamps, but the postal clerk just laughed at me. I had to pay full price. But when I did all the math in my head, I calculated that, if I charged a dollar a postcard, I would make over seventy cents on each one sold. There were thousands of tourists on Fort Lauderdale beach and I figured I could write about a hundred postcards in eight hours, one every five minutes. That'd add up to better pay than any junior rat exterminator's. And it would give me perfect writing balance. Cheerful postcard writer by day, and tragedy-writing novelist by night.

The next morning we helped my parents load up the car.

"Remember," Dad grunted, as he pushed a suitcase toward the back of the trunk, "when I return, I want to see some cold hard cash. If you are going to sit on your butt all day pecking at a typewriter, you better have something to show for it, or you'll be killing rats."

"Don't worry," I replied, and handed him another suitcase. "The way my life is going, I'll have plenty to write about."

"Any moron with two brain cells to rub together can write," he said. "The problem is, getting people to read the stuff."

"I know," I replied. "You won't even read what I give you." That was a mistake.

"Well, that proves my point," he insisted, then lowered the trunk lid. "Your own father can't stand your writing."

Mom gave him *the look* again, then whispered in my ear as I kissed her goodbye. "Take care of Pete. He's been acting a bit unusual."

He is unusual, I thought to myself. So he's his normal self. "Okay," I replied. "Have a great time and don't worry about a thing."

The moment Mom closed her door, Dad tore out of the driveway and sped down the street as though he had just robbed a bank. I guess they did need a break from us.

Betsy snuck up behind me and clamped her hands around my neck. "Have you ever read the book *1984*?"

"No," I squeaked.

"At the end," she said, "the main character is captured and his enemies strap a three-sided cage to his face. Then they fill it with starving rats that chew their way into his brain."

"What do you want from me?" I gasped.

"You take care of Pete," she said. "Show up every night for dinner, do everything I say, and I'll keep rats from using your eye sockets as doorways to your brain."

"Okay," I croaked. "You're the boss." I went limp and she let me drop to the ground.

Two

My first day out I was sitting under a palm tree like some wasted survivor on a desert island with the typewriter on my lap. Above me I had thumbtacked a big sign: POST-CARDS WRITTEN AND MAILED. ONE DOLLAR.

Business was slow. In fact, I hadn't scored a customer all day. I hadn't even seen a mirage of a customer, and I was in a bad mood. Every time I looked up to make sure my sign hadn't blown away, the sun scorched my face and I thought of rats turning my brain into Swiss cheese. I had to make some money before Dad returned.

Pete was sitting next to me. He was so sluggish he looked like a snake propped up on a stick. "Give me a dollar," he moaned, and stuck out his hand. "I want to buy a Slim Jim."

He was like BeauBeau, only with a slightly larger brain. "No way," I snapped back. "Buy it yourself."

"You own me so you have to take care of me," he whined, as if it were a law.

"I own you so you have to work for me," I replied. "Now it is time for you to get your rear in gear. Because if I end up killing rats for a living, you'll be the first rat I kill."

"I just want to buy a Slim Jim, then take a swim, then fall asleep under a picnic table." He pouted.

"Wrong," I replied. "You will do none of those things. You will put your mind to a moneymaking task."

He groaned. His head drooped over to one side.

"Let me explain the number-one lesson of life," I said. "See those people all over the beach?"

"Yeah," he replied. "So what?"

"Well, millions of years ago the beach was covered with fish with feet."

"I don't get it," he said.

"Let me spell it out," I labored, and tapped him on the head. "Once upon a time we were all just single-celled dots in a pool of slimy water. Then we were fish. Then we were fish with feet. Then we were people. And now our next step is to make money. And if you can make lots of money while doing what you love to do, then it automatically means you are a genius. We didn't go from single-celled slime to people just so we could eat Slim Jims and sleep under a table."

He looked at his feet, then squinted up at me. "That's the dumbest thing I ever heard," he said. "No wonder everyone thinks you're an idiot."

I almost slugged him, but it wasn't in my best interest. "Let me spell it out even more," I said. "If fish didn't decide they wanted to walk, we wouldn't be here today."

"You've been out in the sun too long," he cracked.

I was losing patience. "We're growing up," I said.

"No kidding," he sputtered. "Nobody grows down."

"I don't mean that." I sighed. "I mean it's time to make something of ourselves. Take the next step. Make some bucks."

Pete's eyes glazed over. If I were a book, he was ready to close me.

"The point is all about you and me. Look at it this way. Some fish were dumb. They walked in the wrong direction and died. But the smart ones kept walking from one puddle to the next. The same for us. You and I are—"

"Going from puddle to puddle."

"There you go again," I moaned. "Missing the—"

"I have an idea," he said abruptly.

"That's it!" I said, encouraging him. "Evolve. Be something. Turn your idea into money."

"Dad says, 'It takes money to make money,' " he said, and held his hand out again. "I need to go home and get Dad's old Polaroid. Then I'll need ten dollars to get started."

"Started on what?" I asked. "What?"

"It's a surprise," he replied coyly.

"Well, if I'm gonna bankroll your lazy butt," I stressed, "everything you earn belongs to me."

"I'll save you from rats eating your face off," he said, and made a bucktoothed rat face.

That got me. I gave him the ten.

He jammed it into the pocket of his cutoffs, then began to half flop and half crawl across the sand like a fish with feet. After he had gone about ten yards he turned to grin at me. "When I come back, I'll have evolved," he said.

"Yeah. You'll be a newt," I muttered under my breath.

As soon as Pete left I opened my black book and began to wonder what awful things I could write about. I looked around the beach. I knew that beneath the normal surface of society lay hidden the twisted underbelly of life. That's the good stuff I wanted to write about, but everything looked pretty normal from where I was sitting. The lifeguard stood in his orange tower. The tourists were spread out on hotel towels, and after baking under the sun all morning they looked like neon-pink hors d'oeuvres on crackers. The palm readers were setting up their striped tents, and the ice-cream vendors were working the crowd. Nothing looked suspiciously abnormal. I stared at the blank pages of my book and thought, Don't panic, you've always been a magnet for weirdness. Sit tight, it will come your way.

Suddenly a bald guy with a swollen belly and a gold chain around his neck so thick you could anchor a ship on it slogged a path through the sand and stood in front of me. He had on so much suntan lotion he glowed like a freshly glazed donut.

"I want ten cards, dated the next ten days. On each one I want you to make up an excuse why I can't return to prison on time. And make it believable. You know, like my mother died and I have to attend her funeral. Or they're throwing me a parade for pulling kids out of a burning building. Stuff like that. I'm on a furlough and I have to send them to my parole officer. I'll pick 'em up after lunch."

He pulled a folded ten-dollar bill from the little mesh pocket inside the waistband of his stretchy tiger-print swimsuit.

I held out my hand, and he dropped it in. The bill was damp. I'll sterilize this later, I thought to myself as I smiled up at him.

"Make 'em good," he warned me. "You have a nice typewriter. I'd hate to see something bad happen to it."

"Don't worry about a thing," I said nervously, then smiled at him as I recited my business jingle. "You go free, and leave the writing to me."

He marched off, probably to go kick sand on little guys with cute girlfriends.

I gave him ten days of the worst bad luck I could imagine: Sun-poisoning rash on privates from day at nude beach. Stung on eyeballs by man-o'-war. One hundred stitches in foot from stepping on child's rusty sand shovel. Inner tube swept out to sea by rogue dolphins. Needed blood transfusion after wicked mosquito attack. Witness to a lifeguard mugging. Ear infection from sea monkeys. Amnesia caused by heat stroke. Buried in sand while sleeping and left for dead. Needed hip replacement after crippled by suicide surfer.

I closed the typewriter case with a snap. I figured if my postcard business didn't work out I could write headlines for the *National Enquirer* or *The Weekly World News.*

When he returned he read each one, slowly, with his lips moving. "You have a sick mind, kid," he declared.

I was thrilled. "I'm going to be a writer," I said to him. "The sicker the mind, the more money you make." I held out my hand for a tip.

"I'll give you a tip," he said, and ripped the cards in half. "If my parole officer read this junk he'd probably track me down and have me tossed in a padded cell." He flipped the pieces back over his shoulder and they blew across the sand. "Now give me back my ten-spot."

"No way," I said. "I worked really hard."

He stuck out his open hand. "I'll count to three," he growled. "One."

I stood up. "I did what you asked," I said.

"Two."

"I did the best I could. I'm not the governor. I can't write you out a pardon."

"Three!" He lunged forward and pulled the typewriter out of my hands.

"No!" I yelled as he spun around and ran down the beach with the typewriter held overhead.

"Come back with that," I shouted.

I was too late. He waded into the water and heaved the typewriter about twenty feet farther out, past the drop-off. At first the machine, in its closed case, floated and bobbed up and down on the waves. Then slowly it began to tilt to one side and sink, going down like the *Titanic*. I dove for it. The water was all sandy, and it disappeared before I could reach the spot.

I came up for air and looked back at the bully. He was a big single-celled blob that hadn't evolved.

"Let this be a lesson to you for now," he shouted. "I'll get my ten bucks later."

I hated people who tried to teach me a lesson. I was going to say something that would probably get me killed, but at that moment I spotted Pete and my mind went spinning out of control.

He was tapping his way across the beach with a fake blind man's walking stick made out of a painted cane fishing pole. On his face he had a pair of huge wrap-around sunglasses that were tinted so dark I couldn't see his eyes. Hanging from his neck was the old Polaroid camera. He tapped a few more feet, then hollered, "Get your picture taken. Two dollars. Have a lifetime souvenir of you and your loved ones on Fort Lauderdale beach for only two dollars."

No wonder Mom was concerned about his behavior. And if Dad found out about this he'd have the stick and I'd be the rat. "Over here!" I hollered, as I dog-paddled toward the shore. "Hey, blind boy, over here!"

"I'll be right there to take your picture, sir," he shouted, and waved his arms around. "Don't move."

He stirred up the sand with his cane as he clumsily

made his way toward me. I wanted to kill him. But then I thought better of punching him in the head in front of people who might really think he was blind. They'd probably beat me to a pulp, and pamper him.

"What are you up to?" I growled when I got my hands on his shoulders.

He rotated his head back and forth, and smiled widely.

"This is not what I meant by evolution," I said. "What you are doing is criminal. Mark my words," I stressed. "This is going to lead to trouble."

"It'll lead to big money," he said. "See." He reached into his pocket and pulled out a wad of bills. "I bet you don't make this from writing postcards."

I snatched the money out of his hands and began to count. "Wow," I said. "Sixteen bucks." I put it in my pocket.

"Some fish were smarter than others," he replied. "I'm already on my second box of film. Watch this."

He tapped a zigzag path through the beach crowd. I watched as he whacked a few of the sleeping sunbathers on the butt with his pole. They flipped over with a shout and he began to apologize wildly. Then he acted as if he had gotten turned around and began tapping his way directly toward the crashing waves. The people he had whacked saw him as he sloped down toward the water and they ran to catch him and turn him in the proper direction. I didn't hear what he said next, but in a moment he had them all lined up and was preparing to take their picture.

I couldn't stand still any longer. I've created a monster, I thought, a deviant fish with no shame.

I arrived in time to hear him say, "Sing out loud and I can aim for your voice." Then he held the camera up and wiggled it around. One by one they sang like opera stars and, of course, he took a perfect shot. When they saw the result they "ohhed" and "ahhed" over his ability to capture them right in the middle of the picture. He just smiled brightly and said, "It's a gift."

He had a lot of nerve. I thought I would burst their bubble and tell them about Pete's 20-20 vision. But when I saw them reach for their wallets I changed my mind.

"That will be two dollars a picture," he informed them, and stuck out his hand.

"For his operation," I pitched in, and winked.

"I take tips," Pete announced. They shelled out and drifted away. Before I could pry that money out of his hands he said, "Treat you to a Coke and a Slim Jim."

Now, that was impressive. "You've definitely evolved," I said.

"Money makes you smarter," he replied. "You should get some."

Three

The next morning after I got Pete's camera loaded up with film and packed him off to work, I strolled along the beach to see if my typewriter had washed up. I figured if I got to it fast enough I could hose the salt and sand out of it before rust set in. But after finding a lost swim fin, an ice chest, and cracked sunglasses I gave up.

On my way back to my postcard-writing spot I passed a gypsy tent. A sign outside read: WHY SUFFER? TAKE A SHORTCUT TO THE FUTURE. LEARN YOUR MISTAKES WITHOUT HAVING TO PAY FOR THEM THE HARD WAY. FIVE BUCKS.

That was for me. If I was going to make the big money, I needed to get a head start on writing about big disasters headed my way. Little money came from little disasters, and I had plenty of those. Last night Betsy made crepes suzette, which were vile enough, but they were also hazardous. She poured a bottle of vanilla extract on a heap of ice cream and set it on fire. The bowl got so hot it cracked and the flaming ice cream melted over the table and scorched the varnish. It was really cool-looking when it happened, and we were screaming and laughing, but then the table tipped over onto the bassinet and we just managed to get the baby out before the blanket burst into flames.

This kind of thing happened all the time, it seemed, but I didn't think anybody was going to pay me to read about it. Whatever I was going to write about, it had to be worse. A lot worse, and so humiliating no one had ever thought of it before in the history of writing.

I slapped the side of Madame Ginger's tent. A cloud of patchouli incense wafted out. "Hello," I shouted, then began to cough and gag.

"Enter," she called back. "If you dare."

I dared. "Hi," I wheezed. "I want to see the future." I set my black book down on her round table, next to her crystal ball, and stuck out my palm. Madame Ginger held it between her smooth hands. She wore a gold-lamé turban and had little diamonds embedded in her long red fingernails.

"What do you want to know?" she asked fearlessly.

She wore mirrored contact lenses, which made her eyes look like polished-chrome ball-bearings. As I stared into them I saw a tiny reflection of my face. "I want to know about love and money," I said, and waved the cloud of incense away from my face so I could breathe.

"Ahh," she sighed, and threw her head back. "The two most important subjects in the world. The cause of all joy and misery."

This was perfect.

She hummed some gypsy Muzak as she charted my palm with a red fine-point marker and drew stars and half-moons and question marks. "You are a writer," she said.

I placed my free hand over my black book as if I were taking an oath. "How did you know?" I gushed, and leaned forward.

"It is written in your palm," she said, and touched a line. It made my backbone vibrate.

I didn't see what she saw, but that's what I was paying her for. "Will I write about something awful?" I asked.

"Yes," she said.

"I've already written about a criminal who threw my typewriter in the water," I said, bubbling over. "That was pretty awful."

"What I see is worse than that," she said, sounding very distressed.

"What?" I asked. "Is it something with tragic love in it?"

"Yes," she replied sadly. "Tragic, and vastly humiliating."

I was thrilled. The more misery on the page, the more money in my pocket, I recited to myself. "When will it happen to me?"

She stared even harder at my hand. "You won't have to wait too long," she said. "It's coming."

"Tell me more," I said. "I need the gory details." I opened my notebook, took out a pen, and was prepared to write down her predictions.

She began to shuffle through a deck of tarot cards, then laid them out. "Love," she murmured, as she ran her hands over the pictures. "Love, love, love." Then she brightened. "Here it is." She held up the card of an angel, then pressed it against her eyes. "I see a leg," she moaned.

"A leg. Whose?" I asked.

"I don't know," she replied. "I can't give names. Just clues." Suddenly Madame Ginger slumped down into her chair like a deflated balloon. "I'm whipped," she said, and sighed. "A leg is it for today. I need a cup of tea."

"For five bucks all I get is a leg?" I asked. "Can you tell me if it's tall, muscular, skinny, short, thick, bowed, anything?"

She closed her eyes and tried to squeeze out another vision. "I've got it," she said. "The leg you are looking for is upside down."

That confused me even more. "Is it attached to a body?" I asked. "Or has it been severed? That would be really good."

"Don't go getting psychotic on me," she snapped. "You're too young to be a sicko."

I knew that wasn't true. I changed the subject before she had a vision of what I did to BeauBeau. "Anything about money?"

"You have a lot of rodents in your financial future," she said. "Don't ask me why. Some people have a date with destiny. You have a date with vermin."

That depressed me. I could already feel the rats clawing my face. "Thanks," I said. "I'll let you know how it all turns out."

"I'll know before you do," she said, and slumped back into her chair. "If you need more advice, come see me."

"Okay," I promised.

When I stepped out of her tent I took a deep breath of fresh air. I was allergic to patchouli and coughed up a huge yellow loogie. I spit it out behind her tent. An ant walked onto the loogie and got stuck. I watched closely as it slowly drowned. I bet that's how amber is made, I thought. Then I strolled over to the Yankee Clipper Hotel to think about the upside-down leg.

The Yankee Clipper was my favorite hotel because it was shaped like a cruise ship with decks, round windows, and smokestacks. And whenever I sat at the outside patio, on a barstool, with a pair of smoky-blue sunglasses covering half my face, Coke in one hand and black notebook in the other, I felt like a famous American writer, usually F. Scott Fitzgerald, sailing from New York to Paris. He had a brilliant wife named Zelda who went insane and died in a hospital fire. That gave him plenty of tragic material to write about. I didn't have anything that horrendous in my life, but maybe the upside-down leg could lead to total humiliation. That would be awesome.

Pete came tapping by to give me the morning profits. He was a fabulous non-stop moneymaking machine. As long as he was working, I didn't have to write postcards, but could sit around all day waiting for trouble.

"I'm going to the bathroom," he said to me after I turned all his pockets inside out to make sure he had given me every cent.

"Don't aim against the wind," I advised, as he tapped across the patio and went inside the hotel lobby.

I hadn't got any writing done, as I was busy watching a squad of girls practice synchronized swimming in the pool. I figured they were on the bottom of the evolutionary scale. They were like real fish with feet. And then it struck me. Wham! There they were—eight upside-down legs that belonged to four girls. Madame Ginger was a visionary genius. I was wondering how I might meet them when the lobby door opened and Pete came flying out. A security guard stood in the doorway and shouted, "I don't care if you're blind. Don't let me catch you going into the ladies' room again."

"Geez Louise," I muttered. "I can't let him out of my sight." I hopped up and ran over to him. "Now you're becoming a perv," I said, yanking him forward by his ear. "What would Mom say about this?"

"Don't tell her," he begged.

"As long as you just stick with being a criminal I won't say a word. Besides, you'll make more money that way."

"But it was a mistake," he cried, and slapped at my

hand. "I was practicing with my eyes closed and I went in the wrong door. I was whacking my stick around trying to find the urinal and accidentally poked a woman."

"Yeah. Tell that to the judge," I said suspiciously. "Anyway, I need your help, and you owe me."

"What do you want? I already give you all my money."

"I want to meet those girls," I said, and pointed to the pool. "They have upside-down legs."

"I don't get it," he said.

"Madame Ginger said I'd meet someone with upside-down legs and that it would lead to devastating humiliation and shame. That's just what I need for my writing. Now, what do you see? Eight upside-down legs, right?"

"Right. But how do you know which one you're supposed to meet?"

"I'm not sure yet, but let me handle it my way," I replied. "I have a plan. Tap your way over toward the far end of the pool," I said. "The deep end. Right next to the sign that says, SWIM AT YOUR OWN RISK. I'll follow you."

We walked over there and watched. They bobbed up and down, spun around in circles, and splashed water in all directions. They looked like human lawn sprinklers doing ballet. Then they turned upside down and kicked their legs back and forth, snipping the air like scissors. They all looked dangerous to me. If you fell on top of them they'd slice you to shreds.

"How do they hold their breath so long?" Pete asked.

"Practice," I replied. "Now you take a deep breath." He

did. I ripped the stick out of his hand and pushed him into the water. He still hadn't learned to swim very well and went straight to the bottom. Forgive me, Mom, I said to myself, but he'll be okay. I figured he was good for about two minutes before I had to rescue him.

"Excuse me," I shouted toward the girls. They didn't hear me. I cupped my hands around my mouth. "Excuse me!" I shouted again. They kept spinning around, twirling their arms overhead, and spitting like fish.

They couldn't hear me because their bathing caps were pulled down over their ears. And then they turned upside down again. I looked at those upside-down legs. Which one was mine? I had to take a chance. "If my mother punched your mother," I sang, pointing from leg to leg. "What color was the blood? R . . . E . . . D." I took Pete's cane and jabbed the winner in the thigh.

That got her attention.

She stopped swimming and turned toward me. "Hey!" she shouted. "What's wrong with you?"

"My blind brother," I hollered and pointed toward him. "He's drowning!" He was. He had been under for a minute and a half and was probably blue by now.

By then the other girls had stopped, and all four of them dove underwater toward the deep end, where they grabbed Pete and brought him to the surface. I leaned forward and dragged him up over the edge and laid him out on his back.

"Quick," one of the girls said. "Give him mouth-to-mouth resuscitation."

I stared at her. "Me?" I asked.

"You're his brother," she said impatiently. "I don't want to do it."

I knew how to do it. I leaned over and opened his mouth. At the same time I whispered so that only he could hear me. "Just go along with this," I said. "I'm not kissing you." He didn't say anything back so I figured he didn't mind, or he was already dead. Then I bent over and put my lips on his and blew air into his lungs. I pulled away, sucked more air into my lungs, and started to do it again. Only this time he spewed a bellyful of water into my mouth just as I opened my lips over his.

"Ugh," I moaned and jerked my head back. There was other stuff besides water in his belly.

"Ohh, gross," I heard the girls say in perfect harmony. "That's disgusting." They were well trained.

I took another deep breath, then leaned forward and spit his spit back into his mouth. His eyes opened. "I can't see!" he shouted.

"Jerk," I said and slapped my hand down over his mouth. "I told you to fall into the water. Not drown."

He bit me on the palm and I yanked my hand back. "Goober," he said to me. "I wanted one of them to give me mouth-to-mouth."

"You disgust me," I shouted and hopped up. "I don't even know you anymore," I said, totally grossed out by him. "You've changed."

"Evolved," he said, and turned over onto his hands and knees.

"Criminal," I growled. "Sick. Perv." I turned toward the girls and smiled. "I'm sorry," I said. "He gets this way sometimes. Water on the brain."

The four of them smiled weakly, stood up together, held hands, and jumped back into the water. They didn't even say anything to me. But I wasn't concerned with all of them. When they turned upside down I noticed a red dot where I had jabbed the leg I picked. That's the one, I thought. That's my destiny.

I walked back to my chair. I pulled out my black book and started to write. This is great stuff, I thought. The weirder, the better.

"Help," Pete said again. I looked up. I still had his cane, so he crawled across the patio on all fours until he got tangled up under a table and chairs.

"Suffer," I yelled over at him. "It'll make a man out of you."

Four

In the morning Pete and I got up extra-early and rode our bikes down to the beach before the crowds arrived. I went just in case the typewriter had finally washed up. Pete went with me because it was the only time he could take a swim and keep his eyes open.

I held his blind-boy getup and camera, and was picking through the flotsam and jetsam when in front of me a huge mound of sand was beginning to move around.

"Oh, my God," I shouted. "A monster!"

An arm emerged and wiped a wad of sand away and I saw a single giant eye blinking at me. I took Pete's stick and jabbed it right where the creature was sizing me up.

"Argh!" it growled and rose up onto all fours. Then, before I could get my feet in gear, it stood up and shivered like a dirty dog. When the sand flew off I recognized the convict who threw my typewriter in the ocean. He must have been hiding from the law disguised as a giant sand slug.

He covered his sore eye with one hand and stared out at me with his other. "You again!" he shouted. "You still owe me ten bucks, and I need it now more than ever."

"Hurry," I called to Pete as I began to back up.

Pete ran through the surf until he circled behind me and then we turned and dashed up to Atlantic Avenue. I looked for the convict but he gave up on us and was just splashing around in the surf, trying to wash the sand out of his eye. If he had used my postcards he probably wouldn't be having this problem, I thought.

I gave Pete his blind-boy supplies and camera, and a twenty-dollar bill for film. "Go get breakfast at the Cuban-Chinese restaurant and I'll meet up with you in an hour."

"Can I order a dinner?" he asked. "Betsy's cooking really stinks."

"Anything you want," I said. "Knock yourself out. Just be there when I return."

I watched as Pete safely stepped out into the oncoming traffic. Tires screeched and horns blared as he tapped his way across the street. Then I made my way down to Madame Ginger's tent.

"Good morning," she said, as she wrapped her turban in circles around her bald head. "You're a little early." The gold silk was so tight it pulled her eyes up at an angle. She looked like a plump Siamese cat. "I can wait," I said. I took a seat and examined her crystal ball. I was hoping to see where the convict went, or if Pete was spending my twenty on tourist junk. But I didn't see anything except for tiny bubbles of air trapped in the glass.

After she tucked the loose end into a seam behind her head, she leaned forward and inserted her mirrored contact lenses.

"Okay." She sighed, and poured herself a cup of coffee from a thermos. "Now, what can I do for you?"

"I need to know more about the upside-down leg," I said, and shot my palm out. "What's the next step?"

She plucked the five out from between my fingers, then held my hand. "It's not just the leg that is upside down," she said, after a minute. "It's the whole world."

"What do you mean?"

"Nothing is as it appears to be," she continued, and stirred the air above her head. "Everything has a hidden meaning."

"Like what?"

"Like your brother," she said. "He's not blind. And you are not as stupid as you seem."

Not that *stupid* label again! Mr. Ploof was right. The IQ test would dog me for the rest of my life.

"I see a young man in uniform trying to give you money," she said.

"Excellent. I love money," I murmured, as she pressed her fingers over my eyes. "What else?"

"If you need to know more about the leg, you've got to take control," she advised. "Be aggressive. You will have no tragedy, no major humiliation, no money, and no answers to life's big questions unless you go out on a limb." Then she slumped back down into her chair. She was so deflated her turban slipped down to one side.

"What about another clue?" I asked. "Something I should watch out for. Tip me off to trouble."

She thought about it. "Crushed ice," she replied.

"Is that it? That doesn't sound too tragic."

"I must warn you," she said seriously. "If you want to write about tragedy, you have to live it first. Remember, art imitates life."

I shrugged. "Well, I'm ready for anything," I replied.

"No, you aren't," she disagreed. "That's why I'm warning you."

Suddenly she sounded like Betsy. She was giving me orders on how to live my life, rather than helping me to manage it myself. "One last thing," I said, testing her powers. "Does my sister's French cooking get any better?"

She thought about it. "No," she replied. "It just gets more dangerous. Very dangerous."

"Thanks for the warning," I said. I stood up and carefully peeked between the tent flaps.

"Don't worry about that convict," she said, reading my mind. "By now he's all the way down at the other end of the beach."

I walked over to the Cuban-Chinese restaurant. Pete was sitting at a table playing checkers with some kid. "Come on," I said. "Time to make the donuts."

"One minute," he whispered. "I bet this kid a buck I could beat him even though I was blind."

I threw a buck down on the board and grabbed Pete by the shoulder. "One of these days," I said, "you're going to go too far."

By midafternoon Pete and I were sitting at a table drinking Cokes. I was chewing on the ice and feeling very suave. I had a wad of cash in my pocket that was big enough to choke a horse. I was at a cool hotel. I had my black book on my lap, pen in hand, and tragedy was only a hundred feet away and heading in my direction.

On the other side of the pool, one of the synchronized swimmers walked across the patio. She wore a sports jacket that said "Fort Lauderdale High Flying L's Swim Team." She took it off and draped it over the back of her chair before she took a seat. She was the one I was supposed to meet, since she was the one with the bruised spot on her thigh.

"Psst," I hissed at Pete, and nodded in her direction. "Check out the upside-down leg."

He lifted his dark glasses and squinted at her. "She seems too nice to be trouble," Pete said. "Shouldn't she be covered with tattoos or something?"

"Madame Ginger said nothing is as it appears," I said

knowingly. "She could be a killer. I could be her next victim. Now watch this."

I strolled up to the bartender. Earlier he had told me he was a college kid on summer break. I figured he'd know what to do. "See that girl over there," I said.

"That beautiful girl?" he replied.

"Shh," I whispered, and turned my back toward her. "Not so loud." I peeled a couple singles off my wad of bills. "I want you to give her a Coke on me."

He raised his eyebrows. "Is there something special you'd like me to tell her?" he asked. "Something romantic?"

I couldn't say what I was thinking, which was that she had a nice upside-down leg. "You think of something," I replied.

He stuck out his hand. I put a dollar in it. He snapped his fingers. I gave him another dollar. I was so entranced with the girl that if he'd kept snapping his fingers I'd have given him everything I had.

He plopped a couple extra cherries into the Coke, and set it on a tin serving tray. Then in one smooth move he lifted the tray off the bar, up over his shoulder, way above his head, glided over to her table, then brought it down as if he were going to behead her, but at the last second he whipped the tray clean out from under the glass. For one breathless instant the glass floated in midair, and then with his free hand he snatched it and, without spilling a drop, lowered it onto her table.

She looked up at him, smiled, and gently clapped her hands together. I read her lips. "Bravo, bravo," she mouthed.

He lowered his head, then whispered something in her ear. She giggled, then turned her eyes toward me. I gave her a slow, two-fingered salute and my shy-guy smile. It worked. She smiled back and waved her fingers at me, one at a time. Even her fingers were perfectly synchronized. Then I crisply swiveled around on my barstool and returned to my table as I pulverized a mouthful of ice.

Pete was watching me like a hawk.

"You're supposed to be blind," I reminded him.

"Watch this move," he whispered. "I'll show you why fish have feet." He stood up and slowly, painfully tapped his way over to her table. Each time he rammed his hip into a chair or kicked a table leg he let out a whimper until he had her full attention. Finally he reached her side and said, loud enough for me to hear, "Would the lady like a free picture?"

She glanced over at me. I nodded my approval, and gave her my cool, two-fingered salute and the same shy smile.

She smiled back and said something to Pete.

"Then sing loud," Pete instructed as he moved the camera around in a figure eight.

She sang, "Do you believe in magic . . ."

I nearly melted down off my chair. I believed in magic,

but this was too good to be true. I crunched down on some more ice and sent little shards of it darting through the air.

Pete took the shot, pulled it out of the camera, and then quickly took another. He gave her the first picture, then tapped his way back to me. When he sat down he whispered, "Ten dollars for the picture still in the camera."

"Three," I shot back.

"Eight."

"Four."

I got it for five. He pulled it out of the camera and as it developed before me it was as though an entire dream was shaping up into reality. I felt bliss. I felt love. This was not tragedy. Madame Ginger must have gotten her wires crossed. This wasn't about crushed ice. It was about my crush on the girl with the upside-down leg.

I got up to walk toward her. She saw me coming and, just as quickly, stood up and dove into the pool.

"I told you," Pete said when I plopped back into my seat. "Trouble. Nothing but trouble."

I had forgotten that humiliation was supposed to be literary medicine for me. "Time for you to get back to work," I snapped, feeling a bit grumpy. I checked his camera. There was one shot left. "Take my picture," I said. "And I'll change the cartridge."

As soon as Pete had tapped his way back to the beach, the young bartender came over.

"I noticed you are a writer," he remarked.

"Yes," I said, with pride. "I am." I glanced at the pool. She was still swimming.

He followed my eyes. "Would you like me to deliver a special note to her?"

"Do you have her address?" I asked.

"Can't give you that," he replied. "But for a little something extra I can see that she gets it."

"Okay," I said. "Give me a minute." I sat down and wrote on the back of the photo, "I believe in magic." I gave her my address and phone number. "Call me. Ask for Jack." I wanted to add, If my sister answers, hang up and try again. But I thought of Betsy strapping the rat cage to my face, so I didn't write anything more.

When I returned to the bar I gave him the photograph.

"That blind kid sure is talented," he said, admiring the picture. He read the back, then held out his hand for a tip. I gave him a buck. He snapped his fingers. Two bucks. He snapped again. Three bucks. He snapped again. I hesitated. Something was wrong. Madame Ginger said *he* was supposed to give *me* money.

"Just make it five," he demanded. "This is special-delivery love mail."

I blushed, and gave him the money.

"I know this girl," he said. "She's very sweet."

"Don't worry," I replied. "I only write about really sweet things." I knew that wasn't true. But there was a first time for everything.

"Would you like to know her name?" he asked coyly.

"Yes," I replied. "Absolutely."

He snapped his fingers.

I gave him a buck. He frowned. I gave him another.

"This is for her *name,*" he stressed, and then he lowered his voice and leaned a little closer. "And the tragic story behind it."

That gave me goose bumps. I gave him three more bucks. Now I know why writers have to write so much. Tragedy is expensive.

"Her first name is Virginia," he said. "She's named after Virginia Woolf."

"Who's that?"

"She was a famous writer," he said. "She went insane and one day filled her pockets full of rocks and walked into the river."

"Did she drown?"

"Yes," he whispered. He turned to look at Virginia. She was still swimming. "Her parents," he said confidentially, "are very concerned about her fascination with water."

I was wrong, I thought to myself. Madame Ginger is right. This could be a tragedy. I looked over at Virginia. She had stopped doing laps and was upside down with her legs kicking back and forth. Please come up for air, I thought. Please.

She did, and I sighed with relief. I wanted her to live at least long enough to crush me like a bug.

That night Betsy continued to experiment with dangerous foods. No wonder BeauBeau committed suicide, I thought, after Betsy made me eat a butter-soaked, three-pound Monte Cristo sandwich the size of an English–French dictionary. Afterward, she served up a platter of cherries jubilee. She went into the liquor cabinet, then poured half a bottle of mint schnapps on the cherries. "Who would like the honor?" she asked, holding up a box of wooden kitchen matches.

Pete ran to the other side of the room. I grabbed the baby and ducked down behind a chair.

"Jack," she said. "Just before you came home some girl called."

"She did! What'd she say?" I asked anxiously.

She handed me the matches. "First things first," she sang.

I knew what to do. "Stand back," I shouted. "Monsieur Henri shall perform a death-defying feat." I struck a match and flicked it at the dessert. The flames shot up like the Olympic torch and melted a hole in the plastic light shade hanging over the dining-room table.

Betsy grabbed the platter with cooking mitts and whisked it over to the sink. "Don't worry," she said. "We can pick the plastic bits out."

"Well, what did Virginia say?" I asked, standing behind her and breathing down her neck.

"She said thanks for the photo, and that you are very cute."

"Yes," I hissed. "Victory is mine."

"But I worry about this girl already," Betsy said. "Because if she thinks you are cute, then she might think you are nice, and if she thinks that, then she might think you have the heart of a human when we all know you have the heart of a rat."

I didn't tell Betsy she was wrong. Really, I had the heart of a loser. Or at least I hoped so. My literary future depended upon it.

Five

I was crossing Atlantic Avenue when I looked down the road and saw about a hundred baby sea turtles. Every one of them had been flattened by a car. When they hatched out of their nests on the beach, some of them went the wrong way and ended up on the road. Others went the right way and made it to the water. It got me thinking about the difference between real tragedy and fake tragedy. Some people think it is tragic when an innocent person crossing the street is flattened by a runaway cement truck. But that is not tragedy. That is just plain old bad luck. Real tragedy happens to people who are trying hard to do something great, like me, but through some stupid fault of their own, they screw up and everything falls to pieces. Like all the high-and-mighty heroes in Shakespeare who have a tragic flaw and end up dead, dying, or insane.

As far as I could tell, everything was going too well for me. The upside-down leg thought I was cute. Pete was making enough money to keep the rats from eating my brain. And Madame Ginger said the worst thing that could happen to me would be about crushed ice. If I didn't work a little harder to screw things up, my tragic writing was going to look like a rack of Hallmark greeting cards.

I marched over to the Yankee Clipper and took a seat at a patio table. I pulled out my black book and started making notes, when the bartender saw me and came over.

"You know, I was thinking," he said. "About what you could do to really make Virginia feel special."

"What?" I replied.

"When you aren't here and she is, I'd still deliver her a Coke on your tab."

I thought about that. "But I wouldn't be here to watch her drink it," I said.

"That's not the point," he countered. "The Coke is for her to enjoy, with or without you. Believe me, women love guys who know how to give them room to breathe."

He lost me. "How much will it cost?" I asked. I knew how to understand the bottom line.

"Give me twenty bucks," he said. "That will cover four Cokes and tips."

I winced. That was almost a whole day's work for Pete. "When can I speak with her?" I asked.

"I'll ask her," he said. "Don't worry, you're doing very well here. Every time I deliver a Coke to her, she says, 'Is it from that nice handsome young man?' And I say, 'Yes. Isn't he a prince?' She's warming up to you."

"Then let's forget the Coke thing," I said, making a bold decision. "Let's go for broke. I want a date."

"That could be difficult," he said, suddenly cooling on the idea. "Let's see what happens once she shows up."

"Okay." But already I was thinking, what could be so difficult? I'll just ask her myself. After all, Madame Ginger said I had to go out on a limb.

When she arrived I got up and walked toward her. I figured I'd ask her out, she'd say no, I'd be humiliated and have something to write about. Simple. But suddenly, as I approached her, I thought, what if she says yes? What if she's thrilled to meet me? Then I'll have nothing to write about. But then I thought about it a little more and reality set in. She was older. She was well dressed. She had manners. She was poised. She was refined. She had not said one nice word to me, ever. There was no way in ten lifetimes she'd stoop so low as to go out with a rodent like me who had done nothing but buy her a few Cokes, and poke her in the leg with a stick.

I was right. As soon as she saw me coming, the look on her face went from serene to total annoyance. She bolted across the patio and dove into the pool. It was a crushing blow, but it didn't kill me. And once my breathing evened out, and I realized I was just fine, I knew I had not suffered enough. I needed more.

I sat down and was making a few notes in my black book when the bartender arrived. "Don't take her running away from you personally," he said. "She is more shy than you are. Now, let me help you out." I gave him a five even before he could stick out his hand. He sadly shook his head back and forth. "No, no, no," he repeated. "This is a whole new level."

I gave him another five.

"I don't think you heard me," he sang.

I gave him another five.

"I can't hear you."

He was worse to me than I was to the lady with the typewriter. Well, what goes around comes around, I thought. I gave him the last of my fives.

"Okay," he said reluctantly. "I'll see what I can do."

He went over to her and said something. She shook her head and said no. He said something more. No, she said again. I couldn't hear her but I watched her mouth. I was positive she was saying no, no, no.

He walked back toward me with a big smile on his face. "Surprise," he said. "She said yes."

"Yes?" I repeated. "I thought she said no."

"You misread," he replied. "I asked if she could go out tomorrow and she said no, only tonight."

"Oh," I said. "What do I do next?"

He held out his hand.

"How much?"

"Twenty bucks for her address," he said. "But look at the bright side. After tonight you will have all the information you need and that'll be it for me."

"Okay," I replied. "But this is the last money I'll ever

give you." I dug into my pocket and thought, Which is the worse tragedy, his money-grubbing hands or her potential heartbreaking blow?

He snapped the bill out of my hand, and wrote the address down on a piece of Yankee Clipper stationery.

"Be there at six," he said. "She's a fanatic about being on time. Also, she's a vegetarian, only goes to foreign films, and is thinking of becoming a doctor."

"Wow," I replied. "I thought she had a great future as a synchronized swimmer."

He dismissed the thought with the wave of his hand. "Get real. This girl is going places."

There were people waiting for him at the bar so he left. I walked across the patio and down the beach.

I had my hand up, shading my eyes, when I heard Pete scream.

"Leave me alone!" he shouted. "Let go of me."

"You little faker," said an old woman. "My sister is nonsighted and your little charade is a cruel insult." She pulled the dark glasses off his face and hurled them into the surf.

"Help!" Pete screamed. "I'm being attacked." He gave her a couple stiff whacks on the legs with his blind-boy cane.

She snatched it out of his hands and broke it in two over the top of his head. "Criminal," she growled.

"Child abuse!" Pete hollered.

"You deserve worse," she scolded. She had an iron grip on the leather camera strap around his neck. He leaned forward and panted for air as his eyes bugged out like a Boston terrier's.

"Uh-oh," I said under my breath. "Trouble."

"Give me that money," she demanded.

"It's mine," he choked out, holding a few dollars just beyond her reach.

"You stole it from people," she snapped. "It should go to the unfortunate."

Now, when it came to money, I really got worked up. I ran across the sand, leaping over sunbathers like an Olympic hurdler until I caught up to them.

The first thing I did was snatch the cash out of Pete's hand and shove it into my pocket along with my big roll of cash. Once that was out of the way, I was ready for a fight.

"Get your hands off of him," I ordered.

"He's a juvenile delinquent," she declared. "I'm making a citizen's arrest."

"So am I," I said, grabbing her flabby arm and tugging her in the opposite direction. "Lifeguard!" I yelled.

"Let go of my arm, you awful child," she spit out. "Or I'll send both of you to a home for the depraved."

"Let go," I shot right back. "Or I'll send you to a nursing home."

Just then the leather strap around Pete's neck snapped. He shot forward and she sprung back at me. I fell and she landed with her giant butt on my lap. I thought my hipbones were crushed and my legs paralyzed for life. Then she reached into my pocket and grabbed all our money.

"Give that back," I shouted. I gave her a pinch and she hopped right up, and power-walked toward the lifeguard stand.

Every few steps she swiveled around and hollered, "Nasty boys! Don't you mess with me."

A lot of people were starting to watch, and judging by how they glared at us, they were getting the wrong idea.

"You mean old fish with feet," Pete yelled back.

"Come on," I said, and pulled him along.

"Did she get all the money?" he asked.

"The whole enchilada." I sighed.

I didn't tell him I had twenty bucks stashed at home. But that was for my date.

"I'll see you later," Pete said. "I still have some film left I can use at the other end of the beach."

"Well, be careful," I said, still limping. "If she sits on *you*, you're dead."

When I got home I checked the mailbox out of habit. There was a postcard from Mom and Dad. They said they were returning the following day. And I'll be killing rats the day after, I said to myself. I leaned down and looked into the box to make sure there was no more mail. Suddenly a hornet came shooting out and stung me on the forehead. It felt like I had been stabbed with an ice pick. I yelped and ran for the house.

Nobody was home. Betsy had taken the baby next door to swim in the Sopers' pool. They had a daughter, Christine, who had been an exchange student in Paris and Betsy was trying to figure out how to do the same thing.

I was staring at myself in the bathroom mirror. From the hornet sting my forehead looked lopsided. Like Gumby's head. A lump was forming and right at the top of it I could see the black hornet stinger where it was stuck in the skin. I opened the medicine cabinet and took out the tweezers. Then very carefully I moved the tweezers toward the stinger.

I heard Betsy open the back sliding-glass doors.

"Are you home, Jack?" she yelled. She must have seen my black book where I'd tossed it on the dining-room table.

I didn't reply because my head would move. Just when I had the stinger lined up and was about to pluck it out, she pushed open the bathroom door and it hit my elbow, which instantly drove the tweezers tips into my Gumby lump.

"Arghh!" I yelled.

"Out," she ordered. "I have to pee."

"You should have gone in the Sopers' pool," I suggested, as I closed my eyes until the throbbing pain calmed down a bit.

"They put a chemical in their water," she said. "If you pee it turns *pourpre*."

I went out to the kitchen. In a minute Betsy joined me.

"I'm going to make some French fries for a snack," she said. "You want some?"

"Sure," I replied. I loved French fries. Plus, it was cheaper to eat at home. I figured I had money to buy Virginia a snack, but not a whole meal.

I began to set the table. Betsy had a beach towel wrapped around herself and tucked into the top of her suit like a Hawaiian dancer.

"What's the red lump on your forehead?" she asked as she cut up the potatoes.

"A hornet sting," I said, gently touching it.

"You should put some mud on it," she suggested. "That's what Indians do to make the swelling go down."

"Really?" I asked.

"Sure," she said, and poured a bottle of cooking oil into the cast-iron skillet. "Just go outside, mix a little water and dirt, and put it on."

"Okay," I said. I turned and began to walk out the sliding glass door. I thought it was open but it wasn't. I hit the glass lump first and bounced off. Luckily the glass didn't break and slice me into strips, or Betsy would have fried me up, too.

I touched my lump and winced. The pain made my eyes water.

"Let me see," Betsy said.

I turned toward her.

"You better put ice on it first," she suggested. "You can do the mud later."

I opened the freezer and pulled out an ice tray, then began to run it under some water to loosen up the cubes. I wanted to ask if she would ever go out with a younger guy with a lump on his head and near-empty pockets, but was already in too much pain.

In a minute the oil began to get hot. Betsy tested it with a piece of potato skin. The oil snapped and popped and the potato skin turned brown and crispy. She salted the potatoes, then used a wide slotted spoon to lower them into the skillet. You have to have a steady hand because if the oil splashes out of the skillet and onto the burner it can catch on fire.

As soon as she put in the first batch of potatoes there was a low whooshing sound and a giant flame, like a big red flag, snapped up above the skillet. She screamed and jumped back with the hot slotted spoon still in her hand. As I turned around to see what happened she accidentally clobbered me right on my lump.

"Oww," I hollered, and dropped down onto my knees.

Betsy grabbed a glass of water from the kitchen counter and threw it on the fire. An enormous ball of black smoke billowed up above the flaming oil. It looked like a small nuclear explosion.

"Smother it!" I yelled, and lunged forward.

Betsy unwrapped the towel from around her waist and threw it on the skillet, then turned off the burner.

I headed for the sliding glass door. In all the excitement I forgot it was still closed. Wham! It didn't break, but I hit my head in the same spot again. I staggered back. I was so dizzy I didn't know what to do next. I reached out and clutched the back of a chair to steady myself, then everything went black and I hit the floor head-first.

When I finally opened my eyes Pete was sitting on my stomach staring down at me. Betsy was washing the soot off the wall.

"What time is it!" I shouted, and looked at my watch. It was five o'clock. I pushed Pete to one side and looked into the small kitchen mirror. "Oh, my God!" I shouted. Pete had drawn a little smiley face on my lump. "I'm a freak," I cried out. I took a cloth and dipped it into a bottle of Mr. Clean, then gritted my teeth and scrubbed my lump until it was red and shiny as a drunk's nose. I was hysterical.

"What's your rush?" Betsy asked.

"I have a date," I blurted out.

I whipped open the freezer door and got some ice for my lump. I held it on my head as I ran back to my room to get dressed. I slipped the ice into my mouth in order to free my hand and push it through a shirt sleeve. I was stepping into a pair of stiff new jeans when I bit down on the ice. Crack! My right front tooth broke. Oh no, I thought, this is what Madame Ginger warned me about. I ran to the bathroom. Pete was in there with the door locked.

"You're not allowed to lock the door," I shouted, and twisted the knob back and forth. I skinned my knuckles against the jamb and blood started running down my fingers. I wiped them across my clean shirt. "Idiot," I said to myself. "Moron. Knucklehead." Immediately I noticed that anything I said was accompanied by a little whistling sound. With my tooth broken off, the air came out of my mouth funny and it sounded as though I had a very high-pitched lisp.

I ran back to my room and looked in my dresser mirror. The tooth had broken off at an angle, so that I had an empty V shape between my front teeth. I looked like a total ghoul.

I had to do something quick. I rapidly chewed up a stick of Juicy Fruit, then wadded it up behind the tooth and filled in the gap.

Betsy came into my room. "Is your date with that little girl who's been calling? Don't tell me you're dating a third-grader. Are you sick?"

I didn't say a word because I thought my gum patch might fall out. But I wanted to yell, She's not a third-grader. She's very sophisticated. She's a synchronized swimmer and probably knows more about France than you do. But I kept my mouth shut, and my feet moving. I had to get to Virginia by six o'clock.

Betsy and Pete followed me out of the house. I got on my bike and started to pedal.

"Is she meeting you on a tricycle?" Betsy hollered as I turned out of the driveway. "Or is she using training wheels now?"

I looked at my watch. It was five forty-five. I could still make it if I rode like a maniac.

By the time I got to her house my shirt was soaked with sweat all around my armpits and down my back, and my lump was so agitated I thought I could feel it twitching as it grew larger. I ditched my bike in her front hedge, ran my fingers through my hair and pulled a curl down over the lump, then pressed the doorbell. I didn't hear it ring, and no one answered. Maybe it's broken, I thought. I knocked on the door, then stepped back. Nothing. I knocked again, then pounded, and this time the cuts on my knuckles opened up. I stuck my hand in my pocket to soak up the blood. There was still no answer. I checked my watch. It was just six. I peeked in the front windows. Nothing. I checked the address on my piece of paper. I was at the right place.

She's just late, I said to calm myself. It happens. There was a small park across the street. I decided it would be more polite if I didn't wait on her doorstep. So I walked over. I saw some nice flowers a garden club had planted and realized I hadn't gotten her any. I looked around and didn't see the flower police so I picked a bunch of them. When I sniffed them my eyes began to water, and I began to sneeze. Oh great, I said to myself, my allergies have started up. I sat down against a tree and laid my flowers against my chest.

It was the first time all week that I just sat still with my hands on my lap and thought about stuff. I had been trying so hard to make everything work out so awful. It seemed like such a nutty thing to want to do, to force disasters on myself, when there were so many disasters that occurred naturally. Maybe I had plenty of trouble to write about already if I just stopped thinking there was an even bigger disaster around the corner.

I began to count up all the things that had gone wrong in just over a week. I think the fall on my head was a little worse than I thought because counting my mistakes was like counting sheep and I dozed off. When I opened my eyes about two hours later, her lights were on. By then my allergies were so bad I was sneezing, and had trouble breathing.

"Suck it up," I said to myself. "It's show time!"

I walked across the street and pressed the doorbell. Suddenly I let loose with a huge openmouthed sneeze and a great big yellow-and-green loogie shot out of my mouth and right in the middle of the flowers. Before I could shake it off the door opened. It was a girl about Pete's age. "Hi," she said, then began to laugh like a hyena. She covered her mouth, then left me standing there as she ran off and hollered, "Dan! Our friend is here."

I was squeezing the chewing gum back behind my tooth when I heard another girl say, "Darn. I thought we were gone long enough to blow him off."

Then the bartender stepped out from behind the door. "Hey, buddy," he said, "what's up?"

"I'm not sure," I stammered. "I thought I had a date with Virginia."

"You must have come to the wrong address," he replied.

For a moment I believed him. Maybe I did go to the wrong house. Maybe she was waiting for me elsewhere.

But he had only given me one address. I pulled the piece of Yankee Clipper notepaper out of my top pocket. "This is what you wrote down," I said.

He took it from my hand and looked it over. "Wow, I made a big mistake," he said, and slapped his forehead with his hand. Just watching made my forehead hurt as if I'd been hit with a tuning fork. "I gave you my address instead of hers."

Just then the young girl ran up behind him and pushed her way between him and the door. She waved my photograph in the air. "Did you write this?" she asked, then turned it over and pointed at my head. "You don't have that lump in the picture," she said.

Before she could answer, the bartender pulled her back behind the door.

"Give me that," he said.

I could hear the scuffling of feet and figured they were having a tug-of-war with the photograph.

"Ow!" she suddenly hollered. "Ow!" Then I heard her fall to the floor with a slap. "I'm telling," she howled, then ran down the hall screaming, "Virginia, Dan hit me!"

He returned looking a little sweaty and ran his hands through his hair. "For ten dollars," he said, holding the ripped photograph in his hand, "you can have this back."

I just stood there, dumfounded, trying to catch on to what was happening. Why were they all together? How did they know each other? And then everything began to clear up. "You tricked me," I said. "You must be Virginia's brother."

"I'm sorry," he said. "I didn't trick you. She changed her mind and decided not to go out with you."

"You ripped me off all along," I said, feeling all high and mighty. "You and Virginia were just using me."

"Well, who is worse?" he asked, sounding a little huffy. "Me for trying to make a little extra tip money? Or you and your *blind* brother you put to work on the beach?"

He had me there.

"Well, what about the date?" I asked, getting back to the real subject. "Were you just going to let me stand out here all night?"

He pulled his wallet out of his back pocket and removed a twenty. "Here," he said. "This should make up for some of it."

"No thanks," I replied. "I can't be bought off."

"I'm not trying to buy you off," he said. "I'm trying to make you feel better."

"I don't want to feel better, either," I said. I took a big breath and accidentally swallowed my chewing-gum tooth patch. I was horrified. "Excuse me," I said. The words whistled out of my mouth.

Just then Virginia opened the door all the way. "Sorry, kid," she said. "This was all his idea. I told my brother I wouldn't go out on a date with someone I didn't know. But he just took your money and set up the date anyway. He figured I'd go along with it, but *nobody* tells me who to date!" She gave her brother a dirty look.

"I can't blame you," I said meekly, whistling the words.

I didn't know what else to do. I just wanted to get out

of there. But since I had the flowers I held them out and said, "These are for you." They tilted forward like an ice-cream cone and my yellow-and-green loogie slid off and splattered on her shoe.

She glowered at me. "What the heck is that?"

"Whoops. Sorry," I whimpered.

"Sorry's not good enough," she said furiously, and stepped forward. "Clean that off," she said, and pointed at the loogie.

"No," I said, stepping back. "No way. It was an accident."

"You little creep," she said, pouncing at me and grabbing my shirt collar. She yanked me forward. I tripped over the front step and fell half into the house. I tried to push myself up but the little sister jumped on my back and held my head down.

"I gave you a chance," Virginia said from above. "Now lick it off." She raised her black patent-leather pump, with the shiny yellow-and-green loogie on top, to my lips. "Lick it off or I'll squish you like a bug."

It was my loogie to begin with. What goes around comes around, I thought, then stuck out my tongue and slurped it up as if eating a raw oyster out of a shell. It wasn't so bad.

"Oh, gross!" Virginia hollered. As she jerked her shoe back she kicked me on the lump.

"Arghh!" I moaned.

The little sister rolled off me. "That's sick," she said and slapped the floor. "Sick, sick, sick."

"Oh, man," the bartender said. "That is the most humiliating thing I've ever seen, and I've seen a lot of bad stuff."

I turned my head and looked up at him. My eyes were watering and it looked like I was crying. But I wasn't. It was the allergies. "Really?" I asked with a whistle. "Is this really the most humiliating thing you've ever seen?"

"Really," he confirmed. "No doubt about it."

"Then shake," I said. I stuck out my hand and he pulled me up onto my feet.

"Goodbye," I said.

I staggered toward my bike. As I pedaled away I glanced at the three of them in the doorway and remembered my writing motto: A WRITER'S JOB IS TO TURN HIS WORST EXPERIENCES INTO MONEY. I only had twenty dollars in my pocket but I felt like a millionaire.

when Mr. Adolino turned the corner he looked like he was in trouble. We had come to the French Consolute's office on a field trip to look at French landscape paintings and those are the best. But the paintings had been taken away and replaced with THE HISTORY OF FRENCH UNDERGARMENTS.

"Ooo La La," Johnny Greenteeth said when he turned the corner. I began to pick up my pace so I could see because already Mr Adolino was saying, "Don't go in there boys. Don't go in there." Of course we nearly ran him over trying to get in. Johnny G. pitched a fake fainting spell and keeled over as he sighed, "I'm in heaven." I had never seen such beautiful underware before. All the underware I had seen was white. But this French stuff was all silky and colorful. And where my

PART THREE

The Fall of the House of Pagoda, or The Tattooed Toe

underware was held up with elastic, this stuff had all kinds of leather and silver straps and buckles. We only got to glance at it for a minute because a guard came and closed the door.

DEATH ROW

"Feel my pulse," Tommy said when we got outside. It was as if he had just run a mile. MR Adolino got us back on the bus and we went to Burger King and Mr. Adolino let us order anything we wanted. Tommy put one of those paper crowns on his head and ~~hollered~~ SANG "I'm the King of France, and I love to dance, on Sanday's in my undies, without my pants!" Mr. Adolino made him sit alone on the bus while we ate free chocolate shakes and promised him we wouldn't tell our parents, or any other teachers what we had seen. It was no big deal. Any guy who has gone shopping with his mom

One

It was dark. I stood in the backyard and pulled my swim mask down over my face, and slipped the snorkel mouthpiece between my teeth. I removed a handkerchief from my top pocket, poured half a bottle of English Leather cologne on it, then reached above my head and carefully poked the handkerchief into the snorkel tube. I took a deep breath and the rush of cologne fumes nearly knocked me over. But it was better than smelling the fumes of the dead and rotting.

I was doing it again. I stood above BeauBeau's grave and thrust the shovel into the dirt. I looked over both shoulders one more time just in case someone was watching. "God help me," I muttered. I lifted the shovel and threw the dirt over to one side. I pushed the shovel down again. "I didn't mean to dig you up the first time," I said to BeauBeau. I lifted the shovel, flipped the dirt onto the pile, and pushed the blade back in. "Now I have to do it again." I grunted as I lifted a big lump of damp soil. Suddenly it was as if I had pulled the cork stopper out of a bottle of the worst-smelling substance known to man. A fog of nasty-smelling BeauBeau fumes began to unfurl and it curled up around me as I shivered. Then from the mouth of the hole came a string of fearless, red-eyed albino rats. I took a step back. I didn't want any of them sneaking up behind me and running up my legs.

Dad had said I got off the hook from killing rats at the concrete factory because some other dad gave his son the job. But I was back on the hook, and I was mad. I knew these monsters had been feasting off of BeauBeau's flesh and they were gonna pay. I raised the shovel up over my head and brought it down on the one closest to my shoe. I hit it so hard I drove it into the soft earth, as if I were pressing chocolate bits into cookie dough. "Take that, you grave gourmet," I muttered. But then it squirmed around and clawed its way out of the indentation. That spooked me. It couldn't be killed. I stepped back and before I could hit it again it ran back into its hole. When I looked up, there were half a dozen rats crawling around the dirt, sniffing for food and licking my shoes. "Scat," I hissed, and kicked one cleanly into the neighbor's yard. The rest knew I meant business and scampered back into one of their tunnels. I dropped my shovel and ran to the side yard and sat down under a tree. I pulled off my swim mask and snorkel and tugged my handkerchief out of the snorkel tube. I poured more English Leather cologne on it, then held it over my nose and mouth and took deep breaths. I was thinking about the low road, and the high-road in life. It was my plan to take the highroad and do great things. I knew it would be harder, but still it was the road less traveled and would be worth it in the end. But I had slipped, and I was stumbling along the low road with the lowest of low-minded people—the Pagoda family. When we had lived in Fort Lauderdale, before Barbados, the Pagodas were our next-door neighbors. They were definitely the most demented people in the world. Their oldest kid, Gary, had a criminal record as long as my arm. Frankie, who was my age, was psychotic ever since he dove off the roof of their house and hit his head on the edge of their swimming pool. And green-haired Susie was totally out of touch with reality.

And now I had joined the Pagodas on the road to ruin. I had bragged to Mr. Pagoda about the dog coffin. That was a mistake. Now he wanted to see it. If he liked it he thought we could make a lot of money selling them to people who bought fancy pet products. He knew a lot about selling pet products, and had made a fortune on them while we were away in Barbados the previous year, and the thought of making Pagoda gold is how I got sucked into digging BeauBeau back up.

This had all started about a month before.

We were sitting in the living room after dinner and

Mom was reading the *Fort Lauderdale News.* "Look," she said to Dad, and pointed to a section of the newspaper she had folded back. "Mr. Pagoda is running for public office."

Dad looked up from his book. "Oh, Lord," he moaned sarcastically.

"Is he running for something, or away from something?" I asked, trying to be clever.

"It says he's running for District Council on the Anti-Pet-Tax Platform," Mom replied.

"That's what happens to people who can't hold down a real job." Dad said. "They become politicians."

"What's the anti-pet-tax platform?" I asked.

"Mark Woody, the guy who is now in office, wants to tax pet owners an extra registration fee that will go to paying for animals that have no homes," Betsy explained.

"That doesn't sound too bad," I said.

"It's nonsense," Dad snapped back. "Taxes will never even out the differences between the *haves* and the *have-nots.* If it were up to the government, each time you paid to have your shoes shined, you'd be charged an extra tax for barefoot people. If you drove a car you'd have to pay a tax for people who walked. If you had a house you'd have to pay a tax for people who slept on benches. You can't tax all the hardworking people to help out all the lazy losers. That is liberal nonsense."

He had lost me. I thought we were talking about pets.

"It does say that Mr. Pagoda is a Democrat," Mom said, adding fuel to the fire.

"Figures," Dad muttered. He was a true-blue Republican. His dad had been a Republican, and had said, "If an ape ran for President, I'd still vote for him as long as he was a Republican."

One time I was writing a civics paper for school and had asked Dad what the difference was between the two political parties. He explained that if there were two starving Democrats left in the world, and only one piece of meat, they would split the meat down the middle.

"That sounds right," I said, taking notes. "Sharing is good."

"Don't fall for it," Dad objected. "They might share it, but secretly the Democrats are sneaks. As they split the meat you can bet each one is thinking, I hope you choke and die on the first bite, so I can have the rest. Democrats will stab you in the back. But the Republicans play fair and square. They'll stab you right in the chest. Instead of sharing, they'd fight it out so that the winner would get the whole hunk o' meat."

That's why he was a Republican, I figured. They were tough, and not embarrassed to be mean.

"The Democrats," he continued, "are weak. They'd rather share than fight. But believe me, neither party tries to change things for the better. They just feed on greed."

I had used his ideas in my paper and the teacher gave me a low grade and wrote a note asking where I got my nutty ideas. I was too embarrassed to tell her I got them from home, so I said I got them from a TV talk show.

Now, before he could really get worked up about government taxation, Mom cut him off. "Well, let's drive over to the old neighborhood," she suggested.

"Sure," Dad said. "Maybe there is a big cage around the Pagoda property, and they are all under house arrest along with all their stinking show dogs." He smiled at the thought.

We got in the car and drove a few miles from one side of Wilton Manors to the other. It didn't take long to reach our old neighborhood. We cruised up the streets, past the Metrics' house, the Peabos', the Gibbonses', and the Veluccis'. They all looked the same. Nothing had changed. It didn't even seem as if the grass had grown, or new flowers had bloomed. It wasn't that I expected something dramatic to have happened, like everyone building a second story, or painting their houses plaid or polka-dot, but I thought there would be some noticeable improvements. Maybe that was because I was always changing, hopefully growing up and getting better, and I guess I expected the same from the rest of the world. But when I looked out at the neighborhood, it was the same old shabby place, and it wasn't getting any better.

And then we stopped in front of the Pagodas' house. Nobody said a word. There was no cage around their house as Dad had wished. But something had definitely changed for the better. Their house was beautiful. Their scruffy old lawn had been replaced with new sod so that it looked like a perfect hair transplant. All the dead tree stumps had been yanked out and smoothed over. The house was freshly painted in a soft peach. The shrubs and boxwood hedges were crisply trimmed. There was no broken glass in the windows. And there were a gold Mercedes and a huge SilverStream Motor Home parked in the new double-wide driveway.

"Are you sure this is the right house?" Pete asked.

"Check out the roof," Dad said, and pointed. "You can still see the shadow of the red atom-bomb target they painted up there."

"The question should be," Betsy said, "do the Pagodas still live in this house?"

Just then the front door to the silver trailer opened and Gary Pagoda stepped out, yawned, and rubbed the sleep from his eyes.

"Oh, my God," Mom cried out. "Look at him."

All of us leaned to one side to stare out the windows, so that the car tilted. He was dressed only in skimpy French underwear and the tattoos of women and birds and bumper-sticker sayings all over his chest and arms made it look as if he had fallen asleep on the Sunday comics.

"Cool," Pete said. "I want tattoos like that!"

I hope he didn't mean the naked lady on Gary's shoulder.

"The only tattoo you'll get will be from my right hand on your backside," Dad cracked.

"It's not polite to stare," Mom said, and slipped her hand across his eyes.

I also thought the tattoos were *cool,* but after what Dad had said to Pete I just kept the thought of getting one to myself. Dad had an anchor tattooed on his arm, but he had been in the Navy and excused it by saying he was drunk and stupid and young when he did it, and afterward it was too late to change. I wasn't drunk, but I was young and I did worry that I was stupid. But I still wanted one. In fact, I wanted a couple hundred. I had this idea once of getting the world's greatest art tattooed across my back. I'd have the *Mona Lisa, Whistler's Mother, Washington Crossing the Delaware*—all the classics. Except the paintings would be the size of postage stamps, so I could travel around the world as a one-man museum and make a fortune by taking off my shirt and selling people magnifying glasses. When I first got this idea I was so thrilled I told it to Betsy. She replied that if I tattooed a line between all the freckles on my face it would spell out "bonehead from another planet."

"I wonder where they got the money to fix the place up?" Dad asked, rubbing his chin.

"Maybe they sold a couple of those brain-damaged kids to a medical lab," Betsy replied.

"Or just won the lottery," Mom guessed.

"Maybe Mr. Pagoda finally invented something really important," I suggested. "Something that has changed the whole world." Everyone looked at me as if I was out of my mind.

"Well, *maybe,*" I repeated.

"Yeah," Dad said sarcastically. "And maybe one day you'll change from a knucklehead to a rocket scientist."

Here we go, I thought. It was bad enough having to worry myself on the subject, but my family only made it worse. I had just started eighth grade and it was open season again for jokes about my IQ level. And Mom was back to feeding me fish sticks. Now as I gaped slack-jawed at the rich-looking Pagoda house, I felt really dumb. I had always thought I was smarter than all of them rolled into one. But how smart could I be if I was just sitting there in a rust-bucket of a car while thinking, I wish I were a *Pagoda.*

"We better get going," Mom said. "If they see us they might invite us in."

"Yeah," Pete said, and wrinkled up his nose. "And if you breathe the stinky dog-poop Pagoda air in their house you'll be paralyzed for life."

Dad put the car in gear and we slowly cruised down the street and around the corner. When we got to Wilton Manors Boulevard there was a billboard with Mr. Pagoda's giant painted face beaming down on us. VOTE PAGODA! NO PET TAX! it read.

"Hey, Dad," I said, joking around. "For once you and Mr. Pagoda are on the same side."

"That just goes to show you how bad my luck is in this town," he muttered.

No one said another word. The Pagodas had passed us by and we were all depressed. Mom tried to cheer us up by having Dad stop at the Dairy Queen and treat us all to a strawberry dip. But it only reminded me of the time Mr. Pagoda poured a gallon of his experimental cherry-colored sun-block into the swimming pool and made us all dive in about a hundred times. Each time we climbed out, we were recoated with a waxy, pinkish oil which floated on the surface and was supposed to "automatically safeguard the skin," according to Mr. Pagoda. Unfortunately, it made our feet so slick the only way to reach the end of the diving board was to crawl out on our hands and knees.

Two

Two days later Pete burst into my room. "You won't believe this," he shouted, waving a shiny brochure above his head. "You aren't as dumb as you look. You were right. Mr. Pagoda invented something and now they are rich! Look!"

I snatched the brochure out of his hand and threw myself across the bed. THE PAGODA PET PAD was printed in bright red letters across the top. Below was a picture of a dog cautiously staring at a little rug that was blocking its way into a living room which had been prissily decorated with white furniture. It looked like God's living room. Below the picture was an explanation: "Vet Approved. The PAGODA PET PAD is a safe and painless way to correct bad pet habits! Keep pets from entering rooms and off of furniture. Just plug in the PAGODA PET PAD and once your pet receives a few uncomfortable shocks, it will soon alter its problem behavior. GUARANTEED."

I looked at the price. "Eighty bucks!" I shouted. "No wonder they're rich."

I could have thought of the Pet Pad, I said to myself. But I hadn't. I hadn't thought of Kleenex, or toilet paper on a roll, or toothpaste, or tiny screwdrivers to fix your glasses, or back scratchers on a long stick, or Pet Rocks, or any of that stuff. I wished I were one of those people who had just one brilliant idea and turned it into a fortune. Mr. Pagoda had, and now I felt more stupid than ever before.

While Pete was busy telling everyone what he had discovered, I rode my bike over and looked at their house from across the street. Someone had stuck a hand-drawn sign in his yard. PAGODA for District Council—NO PET TAXI! I read it twice before I realized there was a mistake—NO PET TAXI! Then I thought, well, maybe he was against pets riding in taxis, too. After all, he was now a politician so he was obligated to keep saying stuff. And who was I to second-guess him? He was the one with the brains and money.

No matter how nutty they are, I thought, they are my friends. I took a deep breath and threw my arms up into the air as I crossed the street. "Let the Pagoda games begin," I declared, as if I were announcing the opening of the Olympics.

Gary Pagoda was sitting on the front lawn next to a

bucket. I crept up behind him and just stood there. The bucket was filled with gasoline. A small tape recorder was at his side. A woman's breathy voice kept saying over and over, "Breathe deep, exhale. Breathe deep, exhale."

I was a little nervous because the last time I had seen him he'd threatened to stab me to death with his Kentucky Toothpick. Now I was worried that if he was breathing gasoline fumes he'd be really nasty. "Hi," I said, as friendly as I could.

He ripped a match out of a matchbook, lit it, then quickly dunked it into the gasoline.

I took a step back. "Hi," I said again.

"I heard you the first time," he snarled. "I'm concentrating."

He lit another match, then quick-as-a-cat put it out in the gas.

"Is this a good idea?" I asked, just as the silky voice on the tape recorder said, "Now let's make a list of positive images. Kittens . . . clean underwear . . . fresh snow . . ."

Gary made a face and snapped off the tape player. "Don't get all weak in the knees," he said with that bully tone of his. "The trick is to drown the match before you can ignite the fumes. You gotta be quick. If you can dunk ten in a row I'll give you ten bucks. If I do ten in a row you give me five. What do you say?"

That was a pretty good deal. "Can you give me a few warmups?"

"Sure," he said, and tossed me the matchbook.

I ripped one off, lit it, then quickly plunged it head-first into the gas. It went out. I did another, and another, without going up in flames. "Ready," I said, figuring I'd have ten bucks in a few minutes.

"Okay," he said. "You're on."

I lit the first one and dunked it. The second. The third. The fourth. The fifth. I had total concentration. I held the matches two feet above the gas, paused to let the flame grow, then stuck them straight down into the gas. Six. Seven. Eight. Nine. Ten. "Finished," I said smoothly, and tossed him the matches. "You're up."

He took a step forward and stood about two inches from my face. "How much will you give me if I set the entire matchbook on fire and dunk the whole thing?"

He still scared me. "Ten bucks," I said, knowing that if he did it I would still break even.

"Watch this," he ordered. He lit a match, then used it to light the corner of the matchbook. He held it upside down until the remaining match heads went up in a ball of flame, and then quickly he plunged it into the gas.

The explosion was awesome. There was a loud whoosh followed by a wall of red flames and heat. I threw myself back onto the lawn and began to roll over and over. I didn't actually see that I was on fire but I wasn't taking any chances. When I stopped, I saw Gary still rolling. Smoke was coming off his pants. He was laughing wildly when he jumped up and ran around the corner of the house. I smelled burning hair, and touched my eyebrows. They were singed down to a stubble. Great, I thought, now I'll have to draw my eyebrows on like those old movie stars. And if I have to explain to Dad how this happened he'll burst into flames and scorch the rest of my hair off.

I stood there for a minute, spitting on my fingertips and swabbing down my eyebrows while waiting for Gary to come back. But he didn't. The gas was burning a black patch on the new front lawn. The tape recorder had melted down into a blob of molten plastic, and the NO PET TAXI sign had caught fire. A trail of thick smoke lifted up into the sky. I smiled. This was just like old times. The people next door, who now lived in the house we used to live in, were staring out their window and shaking their heads back and forth. I waved to them. "Up your nose with a rubber hose," I sang. "I'm a Pagoda wannabe and proud of it!" They closed the curtains. That used to be us, I thought. When we first moved in next to the Pagodas we, too, thought they were insane. But now I felt really happy to be back with them. And the only reason why, I figured, was that I was just as stupid as they were. The Pagodas were my kind of people.

I took a deep breath and pressed the doorbell. A little speaker over my head blared out, "Whatever you're selling we don't want none!" Probably another Pagoda invention, I thought. An automatic anti-salesman device.

Then it sounded like half a dozen little dogs were barking and scratching the inside of the door.

Frankie Pagoda answered. He had a black patch over one eye, like a pirate.

"Yo ho ho," I sang. "It's your old pal Jack Henry. What happened to you?"

I should have been more polite and said hello first, but I was overexcited.

He stared down at the dogs and kicked them out of the way. "I hurt it," he said quietly.

"How?"

"I was prying open a gallon of paint with a screwdriver when the tip slipped and I drove it up through my eye."

All I could think of was Robin Hood shooting an arrow into the center of a bull's-eye. It made me squint. "Are you blind?" I asked.

"One eye only," he replied.

"Do you have a glass eye?"

"I did," he said. "But Gary borrowed it last Halloween and I haven't seen it since."

"How's Susie?" I asked, taking roll.

"Oh, she's still got all her pieces," he said. "But she's started to do gymnastics so you can bet she'll break her neck or something."

"We saw an ad for the Pet Pad," I said, wanting to change the subject. "Is that thing for real?"

"Amazing, isn't it?" he replied, instantly cheering up. "Can you believe we've made a fortune on Pet Pads?"

I couldn't even bear to think about it. They'd made a

bundle on an idea any toddler with a hairpin and an electrical outlet could put together. I figured that made me about the stupidest kid on the planet. Maybe my IQ *was* low, way low, below the Pagoda line.

"Come in," he said. "I'll show you how it works."

"Cool," I said.

We went inside the house. Everything might have been new, but it all still smelled like old dog poop, and pee, and pine-scent spray. That much hadn't changed.

"We have a Pet Pad on the couch," he said, and pointed at it. "It keeps the dogs from jumping up."

I looked over at one of their yappy Pomeranians. Its hair was standing straight out like a scared porcupine's.

"What happened to the poodles?" I asked.

"Couldn't take the heat."

Frankie bent down and removed a small transformer from behind the couch. It was wired up to the Pet Pad. "Dad customized this pad," he said. "The Pomeranians need a little extra zap because of them already being so high-strung." He turned a dial to a setting that read TEN POUNDS. "Touch it," he instructed. "You'll only feel a tingle."

I placed my hand on the pad. It wasn't very strong, kind of a light shock, like when you hold a nine-volt battery on your tongue.

"Isn't this thing dangerous with kids around the house?" I asked.

"Nay," Frankie replied. "Dad says most people probably buy them to keep the rug rats and crumb-catchers from crawling on the good stuff anyway. Besides, we tested it on a lot of kids and not one of them got hurt. If anything, the kids also figured out pretty quick not to sit on the couch."

"You touch it," I said.

"Okay, but turn it up to the setting marked TWENTY POUNDS. Gary and I made up a game called Death Row, where we take turns giving each other a blast."

I did.

"I'll be the Boston Strangler," he yelled out, and touched the pad. He didn't even blink.

"Your turn," he said.

"I'll be Jack the Ripper," I declared.

He turned up the dial to FIFTY POUNDS. When I touched it my eyelids fluttered and I shook uncontrollably. "Ha!" I shouted when I lifted my hands. "You can't kill the Ripper!"

"Yeah. Now turn it up to a HUNDRED POUNDS."

I did and he touched it. Wham! His whole body jerked back as if he'd been hit with an invisible baseball bat. "The Strangler survives to kill again," he said gruesomely, and lunged toward the Pomeranians. They fled down the hallway. Then he took the transformer and turned the dial up to the last notch, marked with a skull and crossbones. "Your turn, Mr. Ripper," he said gleefully.

I leaned forward and waved my hand over the pad. It seemed to hum, and the little hairs on my arms stood up.

"Don't be a wuss," Frankie said. "It won't hurt you."

I gritted my teeth, turned, and sat on it. Wham! The next thing I knew I was on the other side of the room. I had hit the coffee table, bounced off, and knocked over a bunch of dog-show trophies.

When I opened my eyes, Mr. Pagoda was staring down at me. "Hey, welcome back, Jack," he said. "You okay?"

I lifted my arm and he jerked me up off the floor. "Frankie," he said, "don't overzap your old buddy. We could use him to help us hand out leaflets."

"For Pet Pads?" I asked. I was still a little woozy.

"No," he said. "To get out the vote. Didn't you see the sign on the front lawn?"

"Yeah," I said. "And the billboard, too." Just then I glanced out the back glass doors. Gary climbed up the pool ladder and was shaking his head back and forth to get the water out of his ears. He was stark naked. When he saw me looking at him he grinned and pointed to a red burn spot on his butt. I thought it was a bad time to remind him that he owed me ten bucks. I looked back at Mr. Pagoda. He was dressed as if he were going fox hunting in Ye Olde England. He wore tight red pants, with a little black velvet jacket, knee-high black leather boots, a riding crop, and a black leather hunting cap.

He caught me staring at his outfit. "You like it?" he asked, and struck a fashion pose. "I'm giving an anti-pet-tax speech at the Las Olas Kennel Club. Very upscale voters, so I have to look the part."

Just then Mrs. Pagoda entered the room and blew a few

ear-piercing notes on a little brass horn. "Let the voter hunt begin," she shouted.

Gary opened the sliding glass door. "Did you call me?" he asked.

"Go put some clothes on," she said. "Or get a tattoo on your privates—one or the other."

"Will do," he said with a smile, and closed the door.

Mrs. Pagoda turned to me. "He's doing so much better since the therapy," she whispered. "He doesn't hurt other people anymore. And he hasn't stolen a car for three months."

I was relieved to hear that.

"Knock on wood," said Mr. Pagoda. "Now let's get going. I've got an election to win. We're going to take this anti-pet-tax issue all the way to the White House."

"That's right," said Mrs. Pagoda. "It's taxation without representation for pets."

I looked down at the nervous Pomeranian. I could just imagine it yapping, "Give me liberty or give me death!" ready to make the ultimate sacrifice for its species.

Before I left I asked Frankie, "How come I don't see you at school?"

"Are you at Sunrise?" he asked.

"Yeah."

"I took some tests and they said I was too smart and sent me to Nova," he said. "Did big-headed Mr. Ploof give you the tests?"

"Yeah," I said. I was embarrassed to tell him my scores

but I did anyway. "They said I was average and kept me."

"Don't sweat it," he said. "The same thing happened to Gary. They said he was just average, too."

Great, I thought. Gary Pagoda and I are on the same level. "One more thing," I said to Frankie. "What's Gary listening to on his little tape recorder?"

"That's his self-help therapy," he replied. "Whenever he gets wired up and angry he has to listen to a therapy tape to calm him down."

"Well, it didn't work," I said.

At dinner that night I told everyone I had gone over to visit the Pagodas. "I'm going to be part of the democratic process," I said. "Mr. Pagoda wants me to help him beat Mr. Woody."

"He needs more than help," Dad said. "He needs a miracle."

"Well, he's pretty confident," I said. "He said he's going to take the anti-pet-tax issue all the way to the White House."

"Yeah," Betsy chimed in. "And they'll rename it the doghouse."

"I wish you all wouldn't be so cynical," I said. "I'm working for positive change, and you all are so negative."

"A Pagoda in the White House is *not* positive change," Dad said.

"Yeah," said Betsy. "If you want positive change, you should just stop hanging around them."

"Or get plastic surgery," Pete added.

I stood up. "Just wait," I said. "You'll all want to visit me when I'm living next to the White House."

"Sure," said Betsy. "There's always a line in front of the outhouse."

I turned and walked back to my room. Every time I try to do something positive, I thought, my family tries to run me down. Well, I'll show them. I'm going to be on the Pagodas' winning team.

Three

On my first day back at Sunrise I had seen Gary in my shop class. He was so much bigger than the other kids he looked like a second teacher. I had successfully avoided him for a month, but after he had seen me at his house he came over to my shop bench.

"Aren't you three years older than me?" I asked.

"Yeah, but back when I was a juvenile delinquent I failed a few years in a row, so now I'm making up for it. Let's be shop buddies," he said. "My hypnotherapist said I should stop hanging around *bad influences*"—he nodded toward the guys I had seen him with earlier—"and should be with nicer guys."

"What's a hypnotherapist?" I asked.

"It's a lady who hypnotizes me, then when I'm zonked out she plugs thoughts into my brain with a tape that repeats positive ideas like 'Never hurt people' and 'Play by the rules' and 'Cheaters never prosper'—soft stuff like that. And then when I pop out of my trance I behave better."

I was certain that if I had a therapist she would want me to stay away from guys like Gary Pagoda.

"Come on," Gary said. "Lighten up. I know I've been a psychopath in the past but everyone deserves a second chance."

"Okay," I said. I figured if I really believed in positive change, then it was possible that Gary Pagoda was no longer a killer just looking for a victim.

He stuck out his giant calloused hand. "Buddies," he said. "Now shake on it."

I looked him in the eye. He needed a shave. He had a gold tooth. I glanced down at his outstretched hand. L-O-V-E was tattooed across his knuckles. His left hand spelled out H-A-T-E.

"Okay," I said. I took a deep breath and shook his LOVE hand.

"Awesome," he said. "This is really a breakthrough for me. You're the first non-criminal friend I've ever had."

"Didn't you have nice friends when you were in kindergarten?" I asked.

He thought about it, then replied. "That's one thing I've never been able to figure out. Did I turn them into bad kids, or did they turn me into a bad kid?"

"I guess if I turn into a criminal we'll know," I ventured to say. I was still afraid to say something too funny around him in case he lost his sense of humor and took offense.

"You know what you're going to be doing later?" he asked.

"No," I said.

"Passing out voter leaflets with me."

"I have some other things to catch up on," I replied.

He gave me a stern look and aimed his chin toward me as if lining me up for a punch. "We're buddies now," he said. "Blood brothers." Then he punched me in the shoulder. "My therapist said she wanted me to spend more time with nice kids. And you're *it*!"

Why didn't the therapist just tell him to get a nice pet? Or maybe he'd already gone through that stage and the pet didn't survive.

"Okay," I said. "I'll be over once I do my homework."

"Skip the homework," he said.

"I'm trying to be a good influence," I stressed, and slowly stepped back. I didn't want to make any sudden moves and get him riled up. He might have needed a few more sessions with the hypnotherapist. I was thinking that I needed to get an old pocket watch and if he started to lose it I could wave it in front of his eyes and calm him down.

"You can do homework tomorrow," he insisted. "Today I'm in charge."

I felt as if I had been kidnapped by a lunatic stalker.

"As soon as I get home I'll ride my bike over," I said. "I promise."

"Forget the bike," he replied. "I'll pick you up in the motor home."

"That giant thing?"

He nodded. "Hey, I've had that motor home up to a hundred and twenty," he said. "If it had wings I'd fly it around like a bomber."

I gave him the address. He read it. "You guys sure have gone downhill since moving away from us," he remarked.

Not far enough, I thought.

By the time I got home from school I forgot all about my fear of Gary Pagoda, and instead felt proud that he had chosen me to be a good influence on him. Dad had always said I led Pete astray and gave him a lot of really bad advice as an older brother. And Betsy claimed I was so lousy at running my own life that I should be legally prevented from making any decisions for myself. So when Gary picked me to be his buddy and help him be a better person I felt as though *I* was a better person. And I felt smart. Maybe I'll become a therapist, I thought. I could go around helping people be nicer to themselves and each other, kind of like a Johnny Appleseed of positive change.

I'd just been home for a minute and was standing in front of the open refrigerator drinking out of the milk carton when Betsy yelled out from the living room, "Hey! Does anyone here have a friend who drives the Goodyear blimp?"

"That's for me," I yelled back. "It's Gary Pagoda."

Betsy was so shocked she put her book down and ran into the kitchen. "*You* are hanging around with Gary Pagoda?" she asked.

"Yeah," I said. "He's a pretty mellow guy since he got some therapy."

"Right!" she scoffed. "Therapy for him is eating puppies like you for breakfast."

"No way," I said. "I'm killing him with kindness."

"Well, watch he just doesn't kill you the old-fashioned way—with a knife through your neck."

I wiped my mouth on my sleeve and dashed out the front door before she started to make sense to me. After all, if his hypnotherapy wore off, I'd be his first victim.

The motor home couldn't even fit in the driveway so he was parked on the street.

"Hurry up," he yelled from the driver's-side window when he caught sight of me. "Dad gave me a list of things to do as long as your arm."

I opened the door and climbed into the passenger seat. It was so high up I felt as if I were sitting on top our house. "What's our first stop?" I asked.

"Old-age homes," he replied, and pointed to a list on the console between us. "Dad's political consultant says if we get the retirement vote we'll kick butt. On election day I'll drive all those ancient wrinkle rats down to the polls and make 'em vote Pagoda, or else I'll threaten to drop 'em off out in the Everglades." He laughed a cruel laugh.

"Now, is that nice?" I asked, sounding a lot like my mom.

"You're right," he said, and popped me one on the shoulder. "I won't threaten any of 'em. I was just fooling around."

"Well, that's how trouble begins," I said, again sounding just like my mom. I took a deep breath, and figured it was time to change the subject before I drove him crazy. When I saw a tattoo of a rattlesnake around his wrist, I said, "I'd love a tattoo." That was a mistake.

"Yeah," he said, and took another bite of his teriyaki-flavored Slim Jim. "Let's screw the leaflets until later. I know the best tattoo artist in the South." He pulled a U-turn and we almost tipped over. When he straightened out the wheel he clipped the fender of a parked car. Then he just kept going.

"You know what my favorite show is on TV?" he asked, while picking up speed.

I tightened my seat belt as I thought of the most violent show. "Roller derby?"

"Nay," he said. "Demolition derby. I love watching those cars smash into each other like bumper cars. When we used to steal cars we'd play demolition derby where we'd drive down the street and sideswipe parked cars. It was awesome."

"Did the police ever catch you?" I asked.

"Sure they did," he said. "Heck, they knew it was us. I mean, how many guys do you know that are as crazy as I am?"

No one came to mind. No one even got close.

"See what I mean," he said. "The police knew there were no other nuts like me in this town."

"Where are we going?" I asked.

"Dania," he replied. "All the bikers go to this one awesome guy, Savage Sam."

"I don't have any money," I said. "We can do this some other time."

He waved me off. "Don't sweat it," he said. "I owe you ten bucks for starters, and you can pay me the difference later."

When we arrived at the tattoo parlor Gary pulled up onto the front yard, which was nothing but packed dirt and weeds. A big motorcycle with a skull and crossbones painted on the gas tank was chained to a dead palm tree. We climbed down and stood before the black door of a little tilted house.

Before we could ring the doorbell a tall, nasty-looking guy in black leather pants, no shirt, a handlebar mustache, and a bald head stepped out onto the porch. "Hey, Pagoda, you loser!" he yelled. "They finally let you out of the can. Come on in. You're in luck. One of my appointments canceled, so I have time for a job. Now, what is it you are after?"

Gary pointed at me. "Here's your next victim," he said.

"Well, kid," Savage Sam the Tattoo Man asked. "You got any ideas?" He stood in front of me as if he were some kind of tattoo menu.

I was stunned. He had the strangest tattoos. Over his

heart, he had a tattoo of a heart with a nail driven into it. Over his lungs, he had a tattoo of lungs filled with green smoke. Over his liver, he had a liver inside a large martini glass. He reminded me of one of those plastic anatomy models in school. The kind where you can see through their clear skin and examine all the organs. Only Sam was a model of organs gone bad. He even had a brain tattooed on his bald head, with a little turned-off light bulb in the middle.

"Well," Sam said again. "What's your big idea?"

I'd rather have gone home and cleaned the toilet, or washed dishes, or pulled weeds. That was my idea. Anything but what I was doing. I kept thinking that it was my job to be a good influence on Gary. And if I was doing my job I'd just take a deep breath and say, "I changed my mind." But I knew Gary would just groan and get all grumpy, and Savage Sam would roll his eyes like I was some dumb kid and say, "Wuss. Chicken. Loser. Don't waste my time." Then he'd throw me out the front door.

So I said, "Yeah, I have an idea. In memory of my dead dog, I want a little dog tattooed on the tip of my big toe. The smallest dog ever, like a dog so small it could fit next to Abraham Lincoln's feet on the back of a penny. A dog about the size of a flea, so that if my dad saw it he would think it was a piece of dirt."

Savage looked back at Gary. "So you brought me a challenge," he said, grinning and nodding his dead-brained head.

"I told you I had smart friends," Gary replied, giving me the double thumbs-up.

"Awesome," Savage said as he picked up his high-speed drill and revved it a few times. "I'm up for it, dude." He turned to me. "Take off your shoe and sock."

I did. He studied my toe for a minute. "I'll do my best to keep it small," he said. But judging by the giant teeth tattooed on the outside of his face, the thick arteries climbing up his neck, and a full-size 3-D backbone over his backbone, I didn't think the word "small" was in Sam's vocabulary.

First, he washed my toe with one of those hand wipes you get in restaurants after you eat a lobster. Then he put on a rubber glove. When he turned on the tattoo gun the needle whined like a dental drill, and when he pressed it against my toe it felt the same way, only worse. There was no novocaine. Gary held my foot down on the mat and I bit down on a rawhide dog-chew toy as Savage Sam drew on me. I didn't dare wiggle my toe, for otherwise I figured BeauBeau's face would have a scratch line across it like when you just goof around with an Etch-A-Sketch.

About an hour later I moaned, "Can't you hurry?"

"I'm an artist," Savage replied, somewhat insulted. "If you want something quick, go buy one of those sissy stick-on tattoos that your mom can wash off at bath time." Then he continued to drill me with that needle at a hundred pinpricks per second.

When he finished the dog he asked, "Any name you want underneath?"

"BeauBeau," I mumbled. I was half delirious from the pain.

He snickered. "What? Did you ever have a girl suck on your toes?" he asked.

I spit the dog toy out of my mouth. "No," I said. I couldn't see the connection. I couldn't even imagine it. Why would anyone suck on a toe? Suddenly I thought I had gone insane. Gary Pagoda was now my best friend, we were driving around in the Goodyear blimp on wheels, I was in a section of town that was a hangout for America's most-wanted criminals, I was getting a tattoo from a human-anatomy model who was asking if I ever had my toes sucked on by a girl, and I was chewing on a dog toy. I wasn't a good influence. *I* was under the influence, and I wanted out.

"Can I suggest something like, 'I'm your puppy love,' " Sam asked, trying to be helpful.

"No, just BeauBeau," I replied. "And in cursive."

"Okay," he said. "You're the boss."

Finally, when it was all over he took a step back and admired his work. "There, it's now on forever. The only way you can get that off is with a hatchet."

I was sure Dad had one.

I hopped off the table and hobbled over to a chair. Savage gave me a hand mirror so I could examine the work. Instead of BeauBeau, he had written YO-YO. I didn't say anything—besides, YO-YO was sort of BeauBeau's nickname, and would probably be my name, too, once Dad or Mom or Betsy got one look at my toe.

Then he turned to Gary. "Anything for you?" he asked. "I'm on a roll."

Gary unbuttoned his shirt. "Yeah," he replied. "I been thinking. How about writing in big letters DAD FOR PRESIDENT just below the TAKE NO PRISONERS—KILL 'EM ALL AND LET GOD SORT 'EM OUT! and above the fightin' Irish Leprechaun."

"You want it in American-flag colors?" Savage asked.

"Cool," Gary replied. "He'll really dig this when I whip off my shirt at dinner."

I knew I would never take off my shoe again in front of anyone in my family. That is, if I could ever get my shoe back on. My toe had swollen up so much I could only get my foot into my sneaker about three-fourths of the way. I just crunched down the back of the heel as if I were wearing a bedroom slipper.

As the tattoo drill whirred, Gary and Sam kept up a conversation about old pals, and old criminal times. I just closed my eyes and dropped my head into my hands.

What have I gotten myself into? I thought. This isn't what I'd call taking the highroad.

Four

I was sitting in the bathroom soaking my toe in a jar of warm water. I knew I couldn't get rid of the tattoo, but I was trying to get the swelling to go down and keep it from being infected. Another day with Gary Pagoda, I thought, and I'll be checked into a mental institution. I balanced my diary on my lap and wrote, "Maybe I am really as dumb as Mr. Ploof said I was. I can no longer deny the facts. I haven't written the blockbuster novel I set out to write. I haven't made a fortune and moved to Paris. And even Frankie Pagoda is smart enough to test out of Sunrise. Dad was right. Brains will only get in the way for me. I should build a career based on physical labor."

Just then Betsy yelled my name. "Jack, Jack! Come here quick!"

I hopped up and knocked over the jar of water. I

yanked on my sock and ran into the living room. Betsy pointed at the TV. It was a Mr. Woody commercial. He was holding a Pagoda Pet Pad and saying, ". . . my opponent claims he is anti–pet tax, and pro-pet. But you be the judge." He set the pad on the ground, plugged it in, and a lab technician set a dog on it. Mr. Woody turned the pad on and the dog yapped out in pain, did a little dance, and jumped off. "A vote for Pagoda is a vote for pet abuse," said Mr. Woody, as the dog licked its tender paws.

"Pagoda is finished," Betsy announced. "The Pet Pad is his Achilles' heel."

"Maybe not," I said. "People know that dogs need negative reinforcement. It's no worse than a little tap on the butt with a newspaper."

Betsy scoffed. "If you want to see negative reinforcement," she said, "you should see Mr. Woody's other commercial. He has a senior citizen testifying that he accidentally stepped on a Pet Pad and it zapped the pacemaker in his heart and he almost died."

She was right. Mr. Pagoda was finished unless he had a secret weapon I didn't know about. Maybe he had one more invention to help him fight off Mr. Woody's ads.

That night Gary Pagoda tapped on my window.

I pulled back the curtain. I could barely see him because he had covered his face with black shoe polish like some kind of Marine commando. But the streetlight reflected off his gold tooth and I recognized him.

"Come out," he said. "I need to talk with you."

"About what?" I whispered.

"Just get out here," he ordered. "Dad has sent us on a mission."

Suddenly I was getting a very bad feeling that Gary was Mr. Pagoda's secret weapon. As I got dressed in dark clothes, I wondered what we might do. Maybe we could take undercover photographs of Mr. Woody selling dogs and cats to medical researchers where their hair would be shaved and their heads drilled and filled with wires. Maybe Mr. Woody had a mansion built with the tax money he had collected to help cats and dogs. Now, if we could get those kinds of pictures, Mr. Pagoda would have a fighting chance. Otherwise, he was doomed.

I slipped out the front door, trotted across our front yard, and climbed into the mobile home.

"What's our mission?" I asked, as we pulled away. "Where are we going?"

He removed a cassette tape from his top pocket and pushed it into the tape deck. I expected to hear our top-secret orders from Mr. Pagoda. Instead, a woman's voice came on. It was Gary's therapist. "Gary," she said very calmly. "Close your eyes and breathe deeply. Relax and breathe deeply."

I glanced at him. His eyes were closed, and he was still driving.

"Gary," she said. "Remember to *center* yourself." I wasn't sure what she meant but we were driving down the middle of the street.

When we began to drift toward the curb I reached forward and pressed the button to eject the tape.

"Hey," he snapped and grabbed my hand. "That was helping me focus."

"Focus on the road," I suggested, and pointed to a telephone pole lined up in our headlights.

He steered to miss it, then snatched the tape and tossed it out the window.

"Now, why did you do that?" I asked.

"It wasn't helping," he said, like some weary zombie warrior. "Nothing is going to help anymore."

I didn't like the way he said that. "I was thinking that your dad needs an invention, like a secret weapon that can turn negative publicity into positive publicity," I said.

Gary leered at me. "I'm his invention," he said, confirming my fear. "I know how to wipe out Mr. Woody's lead."

"I mean, is there a button you can push and Mr. Woody's lead evaporates? Something like that?" I said. "Something scientific and brilliant, like a pro-Pagoda brain wave?"

"I'm the button," Gary said. "And I've just been pushed."

I hoped he hadn't been pushed over the edge. But he had.

Now he was driving the mobile home through the streets with the lights off. Then he cut the engine and we began to coast down Wilton Manors Boulevard.

"Where are we going?" I asked.

"Hunting," he whispered.

"For what?"

"Signs," he replied. "When we reach the corner I want you to jump out and grab all of the Mr. Woody signs and throw them in the back."

"Isn't this against the law?" I asked, knowing that it was. But I was trying to remind him.

"This is war," he replied. "You saw those Mr. Woody commercials. A guy like me can't just stand back and take this kind of abuse."

"Don't you think you are taking this too far?" I asked. "We could be arrested and they could send you away for a long time."

"It doesn't matter," Gary said. "I've tried to go by the straight and narrow, but nobody plays fair." He dodged a dog that had wandered into the street.

"That's not the point," I said. "We all know that politicians don't play fair."

"Then why play? I'd rather just do what I want. I'd rather be a political assassin, or a flaming kamikaze."

"I think you're losing it," I said, taking a chance that he might get even more angry. "Maybe we should turn around and try to find your tape."

"Just do what I tell you to do," he said like the old Gary, the one who loved to sharpen knives all day and throw bowling balls off highway overpasses. "Or else."

I could just imagine the evening news with a policeman saying, "We are searching for a suspect who killed a young man late last night. The body has not yet been identified. But there is a tattoo on one of his big toes of a dog named Yo-Yo." Eventually Savage Sam would identify me, and my parents would bury me in BeauBeau's coffin.

Gary tossed me a flashlight. "Now get going," he said.

"I'm supposed to be a good influence on you," I replied, trying one last time to reason with him. "Not your partner in crime."

"Hey," he said menacingly. "If I wasn't here with you, I might set this thing on fire and run it right through Mr. Woody's picture window. So see, you have been a good influence. I'm only pulling up a few signs."

I jumped out of the mobile home and ran into the field where a bunch of signs were nailed to wooden stakes pounded into the ground. I flicked on the flashlight and looked for Mr. Woody's face. I felt as if I were burglarizing a home. When I spotted a sign I grabbed it and pulled it out of the sandy soil. This is all wrong, I thought. Dad might be cynical about politics, but what I was doing was criminal. Then I thought, if I don't do it Gary will take one of the wooden stakes and drive it through my heart.

"Come on," he yelled. "Hurry up. We got a million more of them to pull up by sunrise."

I grabbed a bunch of signs and carried them to the big side door of the mobile home. Gary opened the door and I threw them in.

"We'll burn these later," he said.

We drove to the next corner and I pulled up a few more. When we got to a billboard Gary jumped out of the mobile home with a can of spray paint. He went around to the back of the billboard and climbed up the ladder. When he stood on the platform he wrote MR. WOODY SUCKS.

"Can't you be more clever than that?" I yelled up at him.

"What's wrong with what I wrote?" Gary barked back. "He sucks! That means don't vote for him."

"It does not," I said. "It sounds so immature." I knew the moment I said the word "immature" that I was dead meat. When he climbed down the ladder he ran and lunged at me. I fell over backward and he sat on my chest with both his huge hands around my neck.

"I didn't mean it," I choked out, thinking, Here comes my death.

"I won't kill you 'cause you been nice to me," he said. "But if you say one word to the cops I'll have Savage Sam tattoo 'Jack sucks' on your forehead. So just keep your mouth shut."

"Okay," I croaked.

Then he jumped up and ran back to the mobile home.

I hopped up onto my feet and watched as he coasted down the road like a silent ballistic missile searching out a target.

That was the last anyone ever saw of him for forty-eight hours, until election day.

Five

Mr. Pagoda had another secret weapon. Sympathy. For the last two days before the election he went on television pleading for his son to come back. He even suggested that Mr. Woody had something to do with his disappearance. And somehow he managed to ask for people's votes while the Pomeranians sat on his lap like electrocuted wigs.

"I told you," Dad said. "Politicians will say anything to get elected."

Mr. Pagoda's sympathy request couldn't counter Mr. Woody's commercials. He'd shown an infant crawling across the Pagoda Pet Pad when zap! the tot flew backward like a fish being jerked out of water.

The next day everyone went to the polls. And that evening I went over to the Pagoda house for the election party.

Mr. and Mrs. Pagoda, Frankie, Susie, and I were all

squeezed onto the Pagoda couch watching the TV and waiting for the final ballot results. Right from the beginning it didn't look good for Mr. Pagoda. And an hour later he called Mr. Woody and conceded. In a few minutes all the local news stations announced that Mr. Woody would declare his victory.

As Mr. Woody stood out on his front yard answering questions from the press someone suddenly yelled, "Look out!" Mr. Woody and everyone dove for cover as Gary drove across the lawn in his mobile home, which had flames streaming from the windows. It looked like the explosion of the *Hindenburg* zeppelin we had seen in a history-class movie. The TV cameraman caught it all, even the flaming SilverStream roaring away down the street.

We just sat there. Stunned.

"I hope he didn't hurt himself," said Mrs. Pagoda.

"And he was doing so well," said Mr. Pagoda. "This is really depressing. But I'm glad that thing was a rental."

Frankie looked at me and winked. Then he reached down under the skirt of the couch and removed the Pet Pad transformer, and before I could stand up he gave it a full blast. Wham! All of us were suddenly jolted off the couch and onto the floor. We knocked over the coffee table, the dog trophies, the framed dog photos, and their collection of Avon dog-shaped cologne bottles.

"Mercy me," said Mr. Pagoda. We all crawled away in a daze on our hands and knees as if leaving a car wreck.

Suddenly Mr. Pagoda jumped to his feet. "That's just

the kick in the butt I needed," he hollered. "I'm not finished yet. I'm going to mount a comeback!"

"With what?" Mrs. Pagoda asked wearily. "We're broke from the election, and the remodeling, and the cars, and can't sell any more Pet Pads after Mr. Woody did us in, and God only knows what trouble Gary has caused."

Mr. Pagoda scratched his head. "I need a new pet product to sell. Something new to market." He looked out at all of us who were standing around him. "Now, which one of you has a good idea?" he asked.

And that's where I stepped in like the bigmouthed idiot I am. "I've got an idea," I said. "How about a dog coffin?"

Mr. Pagoda looked at me with wide eyes. "Brilliant!" he shouted. "Sensational! That's a million-dollar idea, son. Why didn't I think of that?"

I was so caught up by his enthusiasm I said, "I have one at home already designed and everything."

"Great," he said, and clapped his hands together. "Bring it over and we'll work on the details."

"We've got to split the profits fifty-fifty," I insisted, striking a deal while it was hot.

He stuck out his hand and we shook. I was grinning from ear to ear. I'm going to be a millionaire, I sang to myself. Then I danced a little dance as if I were doing a jig around a pot of gold.

"Now you've got the Pagoda spirit," said Mr. Pagoda.

About ten minutes later, as I rode my bike home, a police car drove by with Gary in the back seat. I wasn't much help to him after all, I thought. Neither was his therapy tape. He was going to have to straighten up all by himself.

Now, as I sat in the dark backyard, breathing English Leather cologne through a handkerchief, I knew I couldn't dig BeauBeau back up, not for any amount of money. BeauBeau was dead and buried. It was time for me to leave him rest in peace. And time for me to move on.

The weird thing about the Pagodas, I thought, is that our family was like theirs. Not in the small ways, but in the big ways. There they were, having *made it,* having some money and some chance to do something different. Something better. But they didn't. Just like us, they could figure out how to make money, but they couldn't figure out how to use that money to change their lives. Not just by buying a bigger house or fancier car, but changing who they were, how they behaved, what they wanted to become. That was our problem, too. Dad could sometimes figure out a way to make money, but it never really changed us, or solved our problems. And so somehow, just as he figured how to make it, he also lost it. Just like the Pagodas. Maybe it wasn't about money at all. It was all about ideas. About who you were, and what you wanted to do with your life, what you wanted to become, and how much you love being yourself.

I stood up, held my breath, and quickly spread the dirt back over the grave. I tamped it down with my foot, my foot with the dog-tattooed toe. “I’ve changed my mind,” I whispered.

I returned to the garage, stripped down naked, and threw my smelly clothes in the trash. I tiptoed through the house and into the bathroom, where I took a long hot shower to wash everything away. Tomorrow, I said to myself, I’m going to wake up and everything is going to be exactly the same, except for me.